*Lime*

# *Limoncello*

Book 2

Perry A. Simpson

*1st Edition*

© Perry A. Simpson, 2018

Published by The Lemon Zest Project

All rights reserved. No part of this book may be reproduced, adapted, stored in a retrieval system or transmitted by any means, electronic, mechanical, photocopying, or otherwise without the prior written permission of the author.

The rights of Perry A. Simpson to be identified as the author of this work have been asserted in accordance with the Copyright, Designs and Patents Act 1988.

A CIP catalogue record for this book is available from the British Library.

ISBN 978-0-9926478-3-4

Book layout by Clare Brayshaw

Prepared and printed by: Project Lemon Zest

Email: author@simpsonperry.com

Website: www.simpsonperry.com

*Every smile is a direct achievement ...*

## Contents

|    | Acknowledgments       | ix  |
|----|-----------------------|-----|
|    | A Note from the Author| x   |
| 1  | The Dinner            | 1   |
| 2  | The African Grey      | 6   |
| 3  | Lost Property         | 11  |
| 4  | The Letter            | 15  |
| 5  | Mixed Spirits         | 20  |
| 6  | Killing Reality       | 25  |
| 7  | Sportsman's Double    | 29  |
| 8  | Swedish Surprise      | 33  |
| 9  | Desperate             | 37  |
| 10 | Switching Places      | 42  |
| 11 | Aunt Marge            | 48  |
| 12 | Flowers               | 53  |
| 13 | Movie Night           | 57  |
| 14 | Sexual Exhaustion     | 63  |
| 15 | Forties Night         | 68  |
| 16 | Spirit of Christmas   | 74  |
| 17 | The Nun               | 79  |
| 18 | Pepper                | 84  |
| 19 | Drunk                 | 89  |
| 20 | Hair Raising          | 94  |
| 21 | Nines Lives           | 99  |

| 22 | Stomach Pains | 104 |
| 23 | Hot Tub | 109 |
| 24 | Blood Night | 114 |
| 25 | Shredded | 119 |
| 26 | Sisters | 124 |
| 27 | Meals on Wheels | 128 |
| 28 | The Bricklayer | 133 |
| 29 | Squash | 138 |
| 30 | The Coin Trick | 143 |

# Acknowledgments

This project has taken several years to reach fruition and I have had help and support from many friends, work colleagues and family along the way. I would like to thank all those that have given some of their time to help turn 'Lemon Zest' from that distant dream into reality.

A special thank you to Elizabeth McMahon for continued support and help to iron out those little wrinkles.

In addition, I would like the thank the following for the story ideas:

Helen Hupton for the story idea for "The Letter"

Louise Summers for the story ideas for "Hot Tub" and "Blood Night".

# A Note from the Author

Dear Reader,

Welcome to Project Lemon Zest.

Thank you for choosing "Limoncello" as your next read.

Limoncello is the 2nd short story book from the Lemon Zest Project. It contains 30 quick-read stories of mixed genre. Each short story is a quick read, based on a traditional 3-act plot of around 1,000 – 1,500 words.

The stories are short to meet the needs of the busy lifestyles of people in a world where people are always on the move. Thus, allowing the reader to escape reality for a 5-minute read. This book is for those people who, today, have little free time to relax, but would enjoy a quick read while having a cup of coffee or tea. For some, a quick bedtime read before falling asleep. While others may seek relief from the boredom imposed on them while waiting for the bus, train, flight, etc.

Some the storylines from the Lemon Zest (book 1) continue on in this second series of short stories and the characters will evolve with each subsequent book.

Please feel free to visit our website for more information on the books and read the latest on new books. www.simpsonperry.com

I do hope that you enjoy the book. If all I achieve is to raise a smile, then I will be content.

**Perry Simpson**

# The Dinner

Frank's heart rate rose sharply as he stared at the two bags of meat defrosting on the kitchen worktop.

'Which is the one I took out?' he frowned.

He examined each in turn, they look the exactly same.

'But, how can they?' He sighed.

He slumped down, deflated, at the tired kitchen table. He was on the verge of nailing a long overdue promotion at work. It was Mildred who had come up with the idea of inviting his boss and wife for dinner.

"It's in the bag," he remembered her announcing with that uncanny air of confidence that always surrounded her.

'It's in the bag alright, but which bloody one,' he snapped. 'Probably the most important dinner in my life and we could be serving cat meat instead of chicken,' he stuttered.

He rose slowly from the chair and took another look at the bags, hoping for something, anything that would differentiate the two portions of meat.

---

Mildred stormed into the kitchen completely unaware of the crisis that was about to unfold.

'Frank, you're not even ready. Go on, off you go and get changed,' she ordered.

'Mildred …'

'Don't Mildred me. You should have been ready ages ago.'

'Mildred, you don't understand,' he objected.

'Go and get ready!' she howled.

Frank shook his head and made for the door. He knew it was hopeless talking to her when she was in one of these moods. The door made a slight squeak as it closed behind him.

---

He re-appeared to find Mildred hovering over a large steaming pot. She certainly was dressed to impress and determined to make the evening a success. The air was filled with the rich herbal aroma, steam gathered on the kitchen windows and a gentling bubbling sound could be heard as her creation simmered.

'There is some money on the side. Pop down to the off-licence and get a couple of bottles of decent wine,' she said, waving her tasting spoon at the worktop where the bags of meat had been.

'Mildred ...'

'Frank, I haven't got time to argue. Our guests will be here soon and we should receive them together. So, off you go.

'White or Red?' he huffed.

'White, of course,' she droned. 'And, get a move on.'

Frank admitted defeat and left swiftly through the back door.

---

He drove in complete silence. He remembered how it was the neighbour's playful cat that had been the cause of a few very high water bills nearly a year ago. It had been a very stressful time that had taken their marriage to the brink of collapse. As he recalled, it was the very same grey tabby that he accidentally killed with a house brick as it lay in wait for a tasty Koi carp at the edge of his Japanese-styled pond. He had only intended to scare the little bugger, not kill it. At the time, he hadn't realised how very attached his neighbours were to that cat. Without a thought he had swiftly disposed of the bloody brick and hidden the remains. He smiled as he remembered how the neighbourhood had all rallied round to search for this little bundle of joy – a search that, luckily, did not include the contents of the Becker's freezer.

Mildred was true to form as Harriet and Charles Baldwin arrived, first introducing herself and handing their coats to Frank. By now Frank had assigned himself to the fact that he was about to be subjected to an agonising evening watching and wondering as his boss and his wife chewed on what they thought was succulently spiced chicken!

The evening kicked off with a pleasant glass of champagne. Frank couldn't control the sweat leaking from his brow. The thought that they might actually poison his boss and his snobby wife was burning away at his conscience. Mildred was still not aware of what had happened. Too late now, he concluded.

They strolled through the lounge into the very cosy conservatory. A beautifully set table greeted them. Two silver candelabras provided a very romantic setting. The silverware was placed with the upmost precision. They all sat down. The meal started with an Kir Royal Mousse.

'Mildred is really pushing the boat out tonight. If only she knew,' he choked.

The main course was culinary excellence on a plate. Frank could tell that Harriet was impressed. Mildred was an excellent cook, but this was the first time she had presented food in such an elegant way. For a moment he had forgotten the little hitch – the main ingredient wasn't chicken.

*Limoncello – Perry A. Simpson*

'Mildred, I have to be honest with you,' Harriet opened. 'I didn't expect this. The meat is so tender and succulent.' She took another mouthful. 'Simply melts on the tongue.'

Mildred smiled.

Charles acknowledged by gently raising his eyebrows.

'Frank, do you remember that Chinese restaurant on the high street?'

'The Golden Sun?'

'No man, the Shanghai Palace.'

'Oh, yes, what about it?'

'It's been closed by the food hygiene people – They found a couple of dead cats in one of the freezers at the back.'

Frank spluttered, spraying the contents of his mouth across the table.

'Frank,' Mildred gasped.

Harriet scowled angrily at Charles.

'No, no Mildred, my fault entirely.'

Frank was past worrying by now. They were squeezing the last few drops from the second bottle of wine. They continued to eat in silence. Much to Frank's surprise it had gone down a storm.

'Well, Mildred I applaud you for an excellent meal. You must share your secret with me,' Harriet goaded. 'Where did you get that meat from?'

'Here, here,' Charles shouted while staggering to his feet. 'Please raise your glasses for a toast.'

Everybody stood up and raised their glasses.

'Thank you Mildred for a most excellent meal and I wish Frank all the best in his new post.'

They gently touched glasses and took a sip.

Frank continued to look into his glass. He had to admit it did have a rather unique flavour.

*Limoncello – Perry A. Simpson*

Their guests have finally gone, Mildred breathed a sigh of relief!

'Well, that was a success – a job well done, I'd say.'

Frank just sat there shaking his head.

'Frank, what ever is the matter? You have been on edge all evening. You're not coming down with something are you?'

'Mildred, I have a confession to make,' Frank sighed. 'You know the cat from next door?'

'Go on.'

Frank took a deep breath, 'It's dead. I killed it.'

'So?'

'Remember the two bags of meat on the worktop earlier.'

'No, you didn't?' Mildred collapsed into the chair. There was a long pause.

'Which bag was it?'

'Does it matter now,' Frank snapped. 'We just fed it to our guests this evening, Charles and the infamous Harriet.'

'Frank, I may have given it to the neighbours,' she exclaimed.

'What do you mean?'

'Well, I gave a bag to Doreen next door. There was far too much meat for four.'

Frank stood up looked at Mildred, 'You mean … '

Mildred nodded.

*Limoncello – Perry A. Simpson*

## The African Grey

'It doesn't do much does it?' Sheila inquired.

'Well, it's bird. What do you expect?, Maggie countered.

'I thought parrots are supposed to talk.'

'Well, it does,' Maggie replied.

'Get it to say something then.'

'Like what?' Maggie asked.

'I don't know,' Sheila scoffed.

'Well, it has't said a word since I brought the thing home.'

'Maybe, it's homesick.'

'Homesick? It's an African Grey. It isn't even native to the UK,' Maggie snapped.

The trees outside whipped back and forth. The rain fell from swollen clouds, slowly at first, but soon it was washing down the surface of the windows.

'Still, I would feel homesick if I had moved here from Africa. The weather is enough to make anyone sick.'

Maggie said nothing. She paused to take stock, staring around the room. The drab bamboo wallpaper reminded her of a Chinese restaurant. The matching red arm chairs and three-seater sofa had never been her choice. The glass coffee table always needed polishing and the old tatty sheepskin rug reminded her of past erotic moments with Dave. She knew what Sheila meant. She had moved from a lovely one-bed apartment to this dump.

'The man said it would probably take the bird a couple of weeks or so to settle down. He said once it feels comfortable with us, you'll won't be able to shut it up.' Maggie explained.

'I bought the bird as I thought it might cheer Dave up, or at least give him something to do.'

'He still hasn't found job then?' Sheila asked.

'Plenty of interviews, but nothing as yet. You know how it is these days? When you reach fifty nobody wants to employ you,' Maggie moaned.

'Burning down the premises of the last job doesn't help,' Sheila added.

'No,' Maggie sighed.

'Where did you get it?' Sheila asked.

'Get what?' Maggie responded.

'The parrot,' Sheila went on.

'Oh, the parrot. From the pet shop down the high street.'

'I thought he only sold Dutch rabbits and those ugly gold fish with the huge eyes.'

'Well that's what I thought too. The bird was abandoned. Mr Giles said the police thought that it came an escort agency or something.' she continued. 'The Police asked if the shop would try and find a new home for it. Anyway, I asked around, you know ...,' She paused.

A disturbing thought now raised some doubt about having this particular bird in the house.

'Go, on,' Sheila replied.

"Well, I was told that it used to be in the reception area and would welcome their guests as they arrived, but one of the guests starting teaching it obscene words. This upset some of the clients and the bird had to go,' Maggie concluded.

'Really?'

'Apparently.'

'Could be interesting when he starts to talk,' Sheila chuckled.

'Yes, the thought had crossed my mind. Who knows, It might inject some life back into to Dave. He's driving me mad, moping around, moaning about everything. I am

*Limoncello – Perry A. Simpson*

telling you Sheila, if he does shake out of it, then I swear I'll swing for him. All he cares about is his precious bloody football,' Maggie huffed.

'But, you brought him the season ticket.'

'That was to get him out from under my feet and give me a break. Living with him these days is like some kind of slow torture for married women,' she blurted. 'I wouldn't mind, but we're not even married!'

'As a bad as that is it?'

'No, bloody worse!'

Tears began to fill her eyes. She shifted her gaze to the window. There was a long pause.

'Well, it could be worse,' Sheila said.

'I don't see how,' Maggie snivelled.

'Well, Eric is having a secret affair,' Sheila announced.

Maggie turned at looked at Sheila.

'No!'

'Yes.'

'How do you know?'

'I know alright.'

'But, how do you know? Did you catch him at it?' Maggie asked.

'No. He doesn't know that I know.'

'So, how do you know? Did you follow him?'

'No no. He's got one of these smartphones.'

'Yes, Dave has one. They can't be that smart – he curses it and calls it all the names under the sun!'

'Well, there is an app that you can load onto his particular model that copies all text messages to an email address.'

'Sorry, but I don't have a clue about any of this technical stuff – what's an app?' Maggie interrupted, getting rather frustrated.

'It is application or app for short that you can install onto the phone. So, I installed it and had a copy of all his messages sent to my hotmail account.'

*Limoncello – Perry A. Simpson*

'You have a hotmail account?' Maggie gasped.

'Yes and guess what,' Sheila grimaced.

'What?'

'The bastard has only got three different women on the go!' she proclaimed.

'Your joking? Really?' Maggie blurted.

'Yes, but I have to admit that I quietly admire him, coping with three sex-starved horny bitches.'

'Do you know their names?'

'Tina, Lora and Cathy – in short his TLC!'

'What are going to do?' Maggie asked.

'Nothing yet. I thought about buying a pre-paid phone and sending each of them anonymous message from the other. A sort of circular messages between the three lovers,' Sheila laughed.

'Well, let's face it, all men are bastards,' Maggie exclaimed.

Sheila nodded, suddenly realising that she obviously wasn't enough for Eric.

'Well, Dave, just hasn't got it in him.'

'Have you tried wearing some of that seductive lingerie?, Sheila probed.

'Oh yes,' Maggie laughed. 'I am convinced that the only way to get a good shag out of Dave would be to wear a Manchester United football shirt.'

'They are all capable of it Maggie – don't kid yourself.'

'No Sheila,' she snapped. 'Dave eats, sleeps, and lives for football. He wouldn't allow anything to get in the way of that, certainly not some tart with big tits,' Maggie protested.

'If you say so,' Sheila conceded.

'Trust me he doesn't even bet on any of the games. He has never got any money.'

There was an awkward pause. The rain had stopped, faint rays of sunlight poked through gaps in the fragile clouds. The door banged.

*Limoncello – Perry A. Simpson*

'Is that you Dave?' Maggie shouted.

Dave appeared at the lounge door.

'Hello Dave.'

They all stared towards the parrot, who was now pacing up and down the perch.

'Cindy. Big tits. Blow job. Hello Dave,' the parrot continued. 'Good Fuck. One Hour. Hundred quid. Hello Dave,' the parrot went on relentlessly. '50 quid. Rooney. Cindy. Linda. Suck. Fuck. Blow job,' the parrot added.

Sheila and Maggie looked at the parrot and then at Dave. Sheila smirked.

'Well?" Maggie asked glaring at Dave.

## Lost Property

The wonderful start to Antoine Meunier's day crashed into panic when he realised that he has left his Filofax on the plane. He could still picture it wedged in the seat pocket in front of him. He recalled the exact point in the flight that he inserted it, perfectly placed and clearly visible in the seat pocket so that he wouldn't forget it; it was just after the Captain's announcement that they were currently flying at 35,000 feet, at a ground speed of 485 miles/hour.

'We will be landing at Paris Charles De Gaulle, where there is a light westerly breeze, sunny with a temperature of 22 degrees.'

After all, detail was everything if he was to survive in his particular line of work.

❦

Despite the importance of the Filofax, he did not panic in such circumstances. He had been trained for this and his first priority was to recover it as soon as possible and avoid drawing too much attention to himself.

If only he hadn't bought such a huge gift for his daughter's birthday. If only he was like most other regular travellers who always abused the hand luggage allowance, then he would not have needed to remove his Filofax from its usual place at all. Everything must have its place – it was essential.

He started to retrace the morning's events surrounding the handling of the Filofax. He remembered placing it in the seat pocket in front of him and then fretting about it not being in the front compartment of his case. He recalled how he had to wait until for everyone else had disembarked before he could get off the plane.

A smile occupied his face, but only briefly as he suddenly realised that he hadn't left it on the plane. In fact, he had left it at Caffe Ritazza. He could still see it perched on the edge of the little round glass table. This is bad, he thought.

No time to waste. Antoine turned and headed back to the coffee bar as fast as he was able.

Antoine started to visualise the contents inside the Filofax, how it was organised, where the sensitive data was, and so on. He processed all the possible permutations – would they understand any of the content? What will it mean?

It was not some much of a risk of them reviewing the content of the Filofax, but more the fact that he actually had one that was the issue. He had been trained by a master and it had taken him nearly four years to master the art of this particular type of deception. He knew that he was exploiting a weakness of all the airlines, by abusing certain privileges given to those who genuinely suffered from this particular predicament. Yet, it was how he was able to pass practically unnoticed and without suspicion.

─∞─

Elizabeth Gordon's mobile rang, snapping her out of her little day dream. It was a brief exchange with a handsome young Frenchman. Her quick pace slowed to a gentle stroll, until she came to a standstill as she listened intently. She looked at her phone and played the message again. She smiled. Dinner for tonight was on.

*Limoncello – Perry A. Simpson*

As she place her phone back into her zippy bag, she noticed a Filofax on the round table at the Caffe Ritazza. She glanced around to see if it's owner was perhaps ordering a coffee – Nothing.

She ordered a Caffè Cappuccino, then casually sat down next to the Filofax. Curiosity teased her. She glanced round once more, then picked it up.

'Voila mademoiselle.'

The waiter placed the small round white cup and saucer in front of her.

'Merci Beacoup.'

She admired the skilfully crafted rose drawn in the white froth. It seemed a shame to spoil it. She took a sip and turned her attention back to the Filofax. The smell of leather was unmistakable. It was brown leather, very worn with an unusual cartoon elephant logo in the top right hand corner of the front cover.

She slowly opened it to see "M. Antoine Meunier" engraved on the inside cover. Obviously French, she thought. Her mind drifted for a minute as she tried to image what he looked like. She would like Antoine to be about her age or a tad older, tall, dark and very attractive. This was unlikely, she concluded. She didn't know anyone within her generation that had ever owned a Filofax. She acknowledged that the owner of this one had it a long time and would undoubtedly be lost without it. The question was, should she hand it in and hope that it found it's way back to the owner? Feeling uncomfortable with that, she unclipped the popper and opened it. Glancing down at the content of the inside cover, she noticed a short list of contact numbers. Contact in case of an emergency, landline number, mobile number. It was the same number for all. She pondered about what this mystery man named Antoine might sound like on the phone. Probably rude if he was an old Parisian, she thought.

*Limoncello – Perry A. Simpson*

Antoine Meunier was en route back to the small cafe.

Sweat was visible on his forehead. As he raced back to the cafe, he played out all the possible scenarios. Has it been found? If so, will it have been handed in? Will anyone have looked inside? Of course they would to discover who it belonged to. Maybe their curiosity would get the better of them and they would browse through the contents? Hopefully, they wouldn't go beyond the first few pages which contained only all his regular contact details. But what if they did?

The cafe was in sight now. As he drew closer he noticed someone sitting at the very table where he had left it.

'Plus vite s'il vous plait,' He shouted.

The very dark skinned porter almost collapsed as he arrived at the table. He released the handles of Antoine's wheel chair, bending over to catch his breath.

Elizabeth was startled by the sudden arrival of the stranger sat in a wheelchair. She slid the Filofax towards the grey haired old man with the moustache, but couldn't find any words in French or English.

Antoine's heart sank. In less than eight hours he would be sitting opposite this young lady at the dinner table, handing her the birthday present that has been responsible for bringing them together twice in a single day.

*Limoncello – Perry A. Simpson*

# The Letter

'I will miss you so much,' Emma confessed, slowly spinning her wine glass, tears meandering down her pretty white face.

'I will miss you too my darling,' Mark murmured uncomfortably.

He was actually looking forward to having a break from Emma. Emma was ten years younger than him, an attractive blonde with a complimentary figure to match her irresistibly cute smile. Mark was beginning to show those tell-tale signs of a married man, a grey hairs, a pot belly bulge and lapses in concentration when it was most needed. He felt that their relationship had become too intense and he was sure that his wife, Debbie, was beginning to suspect that he was having an affair. Debbie, who was also his personal assistant. This six month assignment would allow things to cool down a bit.

The candle flickered as the waiter swept in to clear their table, leaving only, a solitary half empty bottle of wine in the centre of tiny rustic table.

Another tear plucked itself from her eye and tracking the previous route, ran gently down her cheek.

***

Mark had been gone a month now and although, the time had flown by, Emma was concerned about how their relationship would be affected by Mark working abroad for several months. They had been having a secret affair now for some time and she worried that he might get used to being apart. After all, he still has that ungrateful bitch of a wife Debbie, she grimaced. She glanced over her PC at Debbie sitting just across the office from her. How did he end up being married to someone like her?, she pondered. She is just so dull. Mark is the very sporty type, he works out at the gym, jogs everyday and plays rugby at the weekends. What does she do? They have absolutely nothing in common. He is too good for her, she concluded.

---

Debbie had noticed a difference in Emma of late. She seemed distant at times, much more prickly and short-tempered. Mark on the other hand, appeared to be much calmer when he talked on the phone. It was almost as if he was enjoying being away from home. Maybe, it was more the fact that he didn't need to maintain this double life style, working all hours, while keeping up this obsession with the gym, she pondered. At one time, she foolishly had thought that he might have been having an affair. She had even suspected Emma of being his bit on the side, but then, where would he have found the time or energy for that? Anyway, she's not his type. Despite how little time they had for each other, Debbie had to admit she was missing him. She was pleased that he was finding more time to relax instead of exercising.

---

Nearly six months passed and Emma was counting down the days to her holiday. She had lied to Debbie about where she was going for her break. It was to be a secret week of passion with Mark who had managed to wangle some time off. Emma had been writing a letter a week to him since he had left for Hong Kong, it was something she had fantasied about since she was a little girl. It had been Mark's idea.

⁂

Mark had decided to end the affair after his holiday with Emma. He knew that there was no easy way to do it, nor an ideal time, but he was hoping that he could at least finish it on high note. Emma is going to be devastated, he grimaced. Mark felt awful, but he just had to put a stop to the lies and, more importantly, the deceit. He was a married man and still loved his wife, Debbie, he concluded.

⁂

As they embraced, Emma felt a soft tremor of excitement ripple down her spine. Her legs began to shimmer as Mark took her in his arms. As their lips gently touched, their passion erupted. Being apart had only made it seem like that first time all over again. Self control cast aside, their lust in full flight, the outcome inevitable. Mark and Emma frantically struggled out of their clothing. Partially naked, they rolled across the carpet, each taking it in turn to dominant the other, feet still bound by their underwear. Emma finally thrust herself upon Mark – he just sighed as she took control. Her breasts swung gently back and forth as she teased him to an orgasm. That was the first of many to come, she thought. She rolled over onto her back in submission and Mark obliged. The night was still young – six months was a long time to be apart.

⁂

Emma woke still exhausted, only a sheet covering her lower body. Mark had his arm around her.

'Did you read all my letters? she asked.

*Limoncello – Perry A. Simpson*

*The Letter*

'Yes, I did.'

'Which one was your favourite?' she teased.

'No one in particular, they were all very good,' Mark lied shamelessly.

He was more concerned about how to broach the subject of ending the affair. Last night the sex with Emma reached a new level. He didn't really care much about the emotional stuff, but he would miss the extraordinary physical encounters.

---

Emma rolled back on top of Mark, her long blonde hair shrouding his face.

'What did you think about my proposal in the last letter?'

'What proposal?' Mark replied, looking confused. He gently folded her hair back.

'You, know? She paused. Writing down our ten sexual fantasies involving sex in odd locations, remember?'

'No, I don't remember that. Which letter was that in?'

Emma sat upright, flicked her hair back and looked sternly at Mark.

'In my last letter – the one I sent last week.'

'I didn't receive a letter last week. I assumed you didn't bother as you were coming here for the week.'

'You must have. It was posted a week ago,' Emma replied, standing up and walking round the bed.

Mark sat up.

'So what's happened to this a letter?' He snapped.

'I don't know. It should have got here by now.'

Mark got up to face Emma. They were both looked at each other.

---

*Limoncello – Perry A. Simpson*

Debbie decided to sort through and process Emma's mail. She usually did whenever she went on holiday. A brown envelope caught her attention. She looked at it more closely. It was franked letter from this office. Odd, she thought. She ran her finger tips along the surface of the letter. Debbie looked at the front of the envelope – she was deep in thought.

She recognised the handwriting and the address on the envelope.

*Limoncello – Perry A. Simpson*

## *Mixed Spirits*

Christine Middlebrooks anxiously waited to hear some news. Accident and Emergency was in chaos. Armed Police were everywhere and she wasn't even granted a much as a glimpse of her husband. I don't even know if he is still alive, she grimaced.

Through the gap between two armed police officers, she could see the other man, Biggs. The doors opened and the doctor paused to talk to an agitated man wearing a full length beige trench coat. Biggs just looked at Christine, a big smile on his face, his menacing eyes were wide open and whiter than white.

The hair on the back of her neck tinkled.

He turned his head, mumbled and went into cardiac arrest.

◦◦◦

Two crash teams worked frantically in a desperate attempt to revive both patients in the same room. Terry Middlebrooks and Rickie Biggs had been admitted at the same time and had both gone into cardiac arrest shortly after their admission.

◦◦◦

Christine could not settle, she was worried about Terry. The children were also restless now. Her sister was supposed to collect them nearly an hour ago and there was still no sign of her. She could do nothing, just wait patiently. Her blue eyes now blood shot, dark roots were beginning to emerge in recently permed blonde hair. Her overweight body balanced uncomfortably on the moulded orange plastic chair.

※

'Mrs Middlebrooks?'

Christine reluctantly raised her hand.

The tall, slim, bedraggled doctor made her way swiftly to where she was seated, 'Would you like to follow me please?'

Christine said nothing, gathered the children and waddled after the doctor. They went into a private office at the opposite side of the waiting area.

'Please sit down Mrs Middlebrook,' she said showing her a chair.

'It's Christine. I mean, please call me Christine.'

A Police officer entered the room and stood guard at the door.

'My name is Doctor Charlotte Staines and I am the doctor attending to your husband.'

Christine nodded slowly and glanced over to the police officer.

'Your husband was involved in a serious road accident.' She continued.

Christine nodded, fearing the worst.

'Both your husband and the man he hit went into cardiac arrest and were technically dead for a few minutes.'

Christine looked up at the doctor then at the stern faced, short, stocky police officer.

'We were able to revive both your husband and the other man, but the true extent of any further damage is not known at this stage.'

Christine gasped. Tears formed and hung, poised ready to flow down her cheeks.

*Limoncello – Perry A. Simpson*

'He has several fractures, cuts and abrasions.' She paused to allow Christine to process the information. 'He will recover, but it is too early to establish whether he has any permanent brain damage,' she sighed. 'He is still unconscious at the moment, so we will continue to monitor his condition.'

Christine looked up at the doctor, 'When can I see him?'

'When he returns from surgery. A nurse will take you in.'

Christine nodded slowly.

'Now, if you don't mind I'll hand you over to PC Hicks.'

PC Hicks sat down next to Christine, took out his little black note book and flicked to find his most recent entry.

'I just need to confirm that you are indeed Mrs Christine Middlebrooks of 15 Middle Terrace, Buckley.'

'Yes, but please it's Christine,' she insisted.

PC Hicks continued to add to his notes.

'This afternoon your husband, Mr Terry Middlebanks struck a man, whom we believe, jumped out into the path of the moving vehicle in an attempt to stop the very same vehicle.'

He paused to read his notes.

'The other man was a Mr. Rickie Biggs, who is currently serving life imprisonment for the brutal murder of his wife.'

Christine looked up at the young Constable.

'Mr. Biggs had escaped from a secure psychiatric unit and was on the run when your husband struck him with his car. The details of the actual crash are little sketchy at this point. The investigations are still ongoing.'

PC Hicks closed his notebook and placed back in his breast pocket.

Christine wasn't sure she liked the hidden implications in the young constable's last comment. Terry was a gentle, shy man. He hadn't it in him to harm anyone.

'What did he do to his wife?' Christine digressed.

'It's a bit brutal,' he replied.

'And?' Christine pressed.

'He was convicted of killing his wife after she changed the Television channel. He stabbed her 47 times with a kitchen knife.'

Christine looked up in horror at the police officer.

'There's no cause for alarm, he's going nowhere with this heavy police presence,' PC Hicks said, trying to put Christine at ease.

It was futile, she was already in a state of shock.

---

Some months later ...

Terry was back home, but still recovering from his injuries. He was spending all of his days watching television. Nothing in particular, just whatever was on.

---

Meanwhile, Rickie Biggs had made a full recovery and was back behind bars at the same secure psychiatric unit. Since his ordeal he was a different man. His will seemed to be broken and no longer needed to be restrained. He just lay on his padded bed, motionless, calm, perplexed, shy, and totally disinterested.

---

Christine had noticed some subtle changes in Terry's character, but she wasn't convinced that this was as a result of brain damage caused by being technically dead for a few minutes.

She recalled how Doctor Staines had told her that the reduction of blood flow to the brain could lead to symptoms of cerebral hypoxia. She also remembered that mild symptoms could include reductions in short-term memory and this may result in decreased motor control, loss of consciousness, and even coma or seizures.

She had said nothing about any changes in character.

There was something far more sinister at work here, she thought. She could see the same evil in his eyes, as that of Biggs, as he lay on the crash cart. It wasn't the evil look in his eyes that had made the hair stand up on her neck that day, it was what he actually said, "They may in-prison me in body, but my spirit will soon be free."

Christine bent down to pick up the TV remote.

'Don't you dare change that channel,' Terry snapped angrily, turning to look directly at Christine with a huge smile, eyes wider and whiter than white.

A cold chill rippled down her spin, making all the hairs on her neck tingle. She turned and went into the kitchen. She very quietly placed the knife stand in the cupboard under the sink.

*Limoncello – Perry A. Simpson*

## *Killing Reality*

They were ready to start the next stage. The lights were red. Both cars nudged forward towards the line, engines purring, tuned and ready.

Jack glanced over at his arch rival. He may have pole position, but there are still enough stages left to win this, he thought. The other driver glanced at Jack, smug after successfully winning on their last two encounters. Victory was within sight for the BMW team. The odds were stacked against the Skoda team, but there was renewed hope in the camp, especially now with the new Volkswagen sponsorship. The new owners had changed the engineering capabilities of the car, but not the image. Image mattered. Jack was well aware of that.

Jack knew that it all hinged on his ability to get off the line quickly without stalling the highly tuned Volkswagen engine. The series 3 BMW was poised. It's slick stylish looks and superior engineering qualities had always given it the edge. The dark blue body glistened in bright sunlight. The shimmering heat haze from the tarmac blurred the lines on the road.

Red, Red amber, GREEN. It was go go go!

Both cars tore away from the line. It was neck and neck for the first hundred yards, but then the BMW stole a slight lead.

The other driver grinned annoyingly.

Jack hated him for that. The BMW would be difficult to catch now, he grimaced. He was cross with himself. It was poor gear changing that had cost him this time.

His only hope was for his opponent to make a mistake, or get caught up in traffic ahead.

It was no use, the rebuilt Skoda was proving to be no match for the Superior design of its German counterpart. He had to accept that his team had finally flipped to even think that winning it was possible.

The upside of this little fiasco was that should he win in the Skoda, then the other driver in the BMW would have to go into hiding for the rest of his life. Perish the thought, beaten by a Skoda of all things. Yes, let's go for it, he grunted.

The sudden injection of excitement generated by this thought brushed aside his earlier disappointment. With this renewed enthusiasm Jack was ready to take up the challenge once more, but right now though, he was trailing his rival and hope of winning this stage of the race was still fading.

―∞―

Jack and the Skoda team had recovered well due to heavy traffic; they were in with a slim chance of winning now. Their eyes met once more. Jack determined more than ever, the other driver bright and arrogant.

I'll wipe that look off your face, Jack warned.

The other driver frowned, acknowledging Jack's persistence in his state of the art, cheap set of wheels.

Jack had worked his way through the gears flawlessly. He glanced quickly over at the other driver. Frustration had replaced the cool, arrogant look.

Jack grinned, Not so smart now are you?

The other driver was slowing. Jack switched lanes and he was on Jack's tail for the first time. He flicked his head right, then to his left, craning his neck to see what his opponent was doing.

Yes, he chuckled. Excitement welled up inside of him. That little slip had cost the BMW team. He relaxed a moment to enjoy the steady pace to the end of the next stage. The BMW was still way back in the distance.

Just when Jack began to scoff, he caught a glimpse of the glistening blue body of the BMW in his mirror. The Skoda eased away. But the BMW continued to hug his tail. As hard as he tried Jack was unable to shake off his opponent. The other driver was well aware of the threat now posed by the up and coming Skoda variant. The BMW hung on as the road curved, waiting for that opportunity to regain the lead. The other driver pulled level, but had to pull back in at the next bend.

The other driver waited patiently for his moment. Sweat formed on Jack's face and his sticky hands gripped the stirring wheel.

I may still have a slim lead, but the other driver still had the element of surprise. It was all about timing now, Jack concluded. The other driver could leave it no longer and pulled out rapidly, drawing parallel with Jack.

Their eyes met once more. Panic started to consume Jack.

Teeth gritted with determination, the other driver made his move in an attempt to snatch the lead on the home stretch. Bit by bit, inch by inch the BMW edged forward. The other driver's tactical recovery plan was working.

The Skoda was on the limit now. Any more and his engine would blow. Jack had almost tasted glory.

The other driver clenched his fist in victory. He had risen to the challenge immediately and the BMW blasted past Jack's car. The tail lights quickly shrank in size as the other driver established a clear lead. In less than a minute the BMW was out of site.

*Limoncello – Perry A. Simpson*

Jack's heart sank. Not only was he going to lose, but it was going to be a humiliating defeat. To add insult to injury the traffic suddenly slowed up and eventually ground to a halt. That's it then, Jack conceded.

---

Jack found himself jostling for position. In his mirror he could see the flashing light approaching.

Something was wrong ahead, he thought. As the car slowed, he could see it was an accident.

Debris was strewn across the road. As the Skoda inched slowly forward he recognised the cracked number plate lying on the road. Jack could make out other distinctive BMW parts. A still body lay in a pool of blood on the road, next to him, a crumpled plastic steering wheel. It was the other boy, motionless and limp. He couldn't see his face, but he did recognise the little boy's bright yellow Nike sweatshirt. Two paramedics worked frantically to revive him. They covered him with an orange blanket and swiftly wheeled him to the back of the ambulance and loaded him in.

Every second counted now. Jack knew that. If only he had worn his seat belt, Jack thought. Dad had also been very strict about that. His thoughts were consumed with guilt and his heart was not filled with envy, but hope for the other little boy.

---

'Sorry you had to see that Jack,' his father said peering back through gap in the front seats.

Jack put his toy steering wheel on the seat beside him and reached for his colouring book. He was no longer in the mood pretending to be a racing driver.

*Limoncello – Perry A. Simpson*

# Sportsman's Double

Angus Baxter sat alone at the bar with his latest best friend, a glass of Jim Beam. 'It was the lack of sex that has driven me to this,' he grimaced. 'I have given everything I have to my 20 years of marriage to Alice and for what? he smirked. Well, tonight I feel like a need a night off from being the perfect and devoted husband, I have needs. I need a shag and tonight is going to my lucky night.'

He sank the remainder of his glass. He glanced along to the end of the bar where a middle-aged blonde had acknowledged him on several occasions already.

---

Angus now had enough courage to slide along the bar to join this very voluptuous blonde, with slate-blue eyes, pale complexion, and make-up beautifully disguising her age.

'Can I get you a drink?' he asked politely.

'Mais bien sûr,' she replied, smiling invitingly. 'A Gin tonic.'

Her voice was very soft which complemented her very distinctive accent.

Angus placed the order for the drinks and slipped along the shiny oak top bar, closer to the mystery women. They had been exchanging glances for the past hour. A stocky bald barman placed the drinks down. He sighed, but said nothing.

Angus raised his glass, 'My name is Angus and you?'

'Je suis Gilberte Petit,' she announced, touching his glass with hers. She winked and threw it down in as single shot.

Angus was taken aback, but felt obligated to do the same and threw down his fifth Jim Beam. It seemed that he was not going to enjoy the taste of this distinctly bold bourbon with its smooth finish and rich oak flavour, made using a secret recipe for more than 200 years, unleashed from deep inside the barrel.

'No, no allow me,' she insisted, ordering the next round.

Another couple of rounds like this and he will be incapable of performing at his best in the bedroom.

Gilberte crossed her legs advertising the fact that she was wearing no panties, 'So, do you fancy going somewhere quiet where we would be alone to ...,' she said pausing to find the right word.

Her nipples stood out, very pert and obvious in her tight white top. Angus felt an awkward bulge in his groin. He really fancied her and he was up for a taste of adultery. She looks 20 years older than me, but she is gorgeous, he thought.

Gilberte slowly opened her legs to allow him to see her shaven pussy.

He looked up at her, stunned and obvious horny.

She very slowly placed her tongue at the corner of her mouth and then sensually licked her upper lip.

'I sense that you're a man for a bit of adventure. How do you fancy a Sportman's double?' she teased.

Angus was gobsmacked. He was sitting with a gorgeous French goddess and now she was offering a threesome with her daughter. Suddenly the alcohol in his body was not proving to be a disadvantage. Oh, yes, I have struck gold here, but wait, he thought. This all seems too good to be true. What's the catch? he asked himself. At that point, a very sick thought crossed his mind, what if Gilberte is the

*Limoncello – Perry A. Simpson*

daughter? That would mean her mother would be what? In her seventies or eighties, he postulated.

'I sent Emma a message, she will be ready by the time we get back,' she smiled.

Gilbert placed her soft delicate little hands on his knee and slid it slowly up the inside of his thigh.

Angus was trapped. He really wanted a night of passion with this stunning French goddess, but the dilemma was how does he get out of shagging her wrinkly old Mother?

'I think we should go. Now that you have made me all wet,' she proclaimed glancing downwards.

Angus threw down the remainder of the bourbon and they left, her arms around his neck, while he supported her upper body. The taxi ride was a mesh of uncoordinated fondles and kisses.

Angus had to keep breaking free for air.

They staggered up a short front stoop and into the house. Angus had no idea where he was at all. It was dark and Gilberte was on fire, kissing him all over. She suddenly stopped and popped out her left breast. Angus obliged by gently licking the nipple until it hardened. She then guided his other hand up between her thighs until she heard him gasp. He didn't know, but his trousers fell to the ground and Gilerte positioned herself so that Angus could make his grand entrance. He forced her back against the wall and she responded by wrapping her slender legs around his waist.

He didn't last long. It had been awhile!

'Now it's time for you to meet Emma,' she chuckled.

Panic started to set in – the thought of sex with the wrinkly old mother suddenly made him feel sick. Brewers droop came raging back.

'She's waiting for you through the door just over there,' she announced.

Angus staggered across the dark landing area towards the nearest door he could make out. He struggled with

*Limoncello – Perry A. Simpson*

the door handle, but the door eventually opened. 'God,' he gasped. He could just make out a glass bearing a pair dentures on the bed side unit.

'Not this room, the other one. I do not think my mother would appreciate sex at the age of eighty-five years old.'

There is a daughter, he thought.

He was feeling somewhat relieved, he pulls Gilberte close to him and they collapsed in a heap on the floor. They both giggled.

Their lips met once more and Angus felt himself stiffening in the groin once more. He wanted to make love to her again on the floor, but she politely withdrew.

'No, no save yourself. Emma awaits behind that door,' she grinned pointing to towards the door opposite. 'Our little threesome remember?'

Angus did indeed. He eagerly got to his feet, offering her a helping hand.

She led him to the door, knocked gently, turned the handle and led him across the threshold.

'Angus allow me to introduce you to my daughter, Emma.'

He froze. The only part that moved was his jaw as it slowly dropped. In front stood a very short, overweight lady dressed in a bulging tight-fitting cat women outfit complete with eye mask and pointed ears! His eyes followed the perimeter of the room and its array of whips, chains, leather straps, and gadgets that he imagined could only inflict pain not pleasure.

He was speechless.

'Enjoy.' Gilberte waved as she crossed the landing.

*Limoncello – Perry A. Simpson*

## Swedish Surprise

Andy Pen knew that his work colleague, Dave Ives, had been looking forward to the trip to Sweden. He wondered what culinary delight he would be exposed to this time.

He remembered their previous disastrous culinary experience in Madrid and thought that Dave might have learned his lesson. Here we go again, he thought.

Andy and Dave were stood at the bar with Lennardt, their host for the evening. Andy had a choice of spending the rest of the evening in the bar with the nice Swedish lady or join Lennardt and Dave for a Swedish surprise.

∽∞∽

'So go on Dave tell me, what is this Swedish Surprise?'

'Well, it's obvious isn't it?' Dave smiled.

'No.'

'Well, it has to be a visit to a Swedish brothel.'

Andy laughed, 'Come on. Don't be daft. Lennardt wouldn't take us somewhere like that.'

Lennardt brought over another round of drinks.

'Well Andy my friend, have you decided what you would like to do? Do you want the Swedish surprise or would like to stay here with the beautiful Swedish lady at the bar?'

'Right now Lennardt I am going to enjoy my drink.'

'OK Andy, we have plenty of time. Our driver will not be here for another 20 minutes.'

The snow had started to fall again. Andy was comfortable here in the hotel bar. The lady at the bar would only provide a good excuse not go with Dave on one of his insane quests. He knew that he would have no choice in the matter. Right now he wanted to avoid any more pickled herring or sill, spicy meat balls or köttbullar.

Of course, Dave was in culinary heaven. He grimaced. Although, he was a little wary about tucking into the meat balls after the Madrid fiasco.

'Have you thought what the Swedish surprise might be?' Lennardt laughed.

He headed for the bar to get another round of drinks, conveniently leaving Dave and Andy alone.

'Andy my son, I think we going to strike gold tonight,' Dave said rubbing his hands together. 'Just imagine having a nice Swedish blonde sat on your lap or better still with your face in her cleavage.'

Andy was already imagining all sorts of awkward and embarrassing moments involving a thong, bra and knowing Dave, there will be wig in there somewhere.

'What makes you think they are taking us to a brothel.'

'It obvious, what else could it be? There's nothing else here except bars and restaurants. In the three months we have been coming here we've done them all at least twice,' he exclaimed. 'Anyway, I have been ribbing Lennardt all last week about going somewhere special – Make it a surprise I said to him.'

Andy glanced over at the nice Swedish lady to take one last look, before being dragged off on another one of Dave's mad adventures.

'Well?'

'Well what?'

'Are you coming with us Andy?' he pushed.

Andy felt obligated and reluctantly nodded.

'That's the spirit. You won't regret it.'

*Limoncello – Perry A. Simpson*

○○○

'Our driver is here,' Lennardt announced. 'This way gentlemen.' He led them out into the reception area, where a very smartly dressed driver greeted them.

Dave winked at Andy. Large flakes of snow continued to smother everything as he led them across the slippery courtyard to a mini bus.

'Still think this is going to be a trip to a brothel?' He said, looking at their chariot – a tatty mini-bus.

'Yes, it has to be. This is probably a concierge service from the club. Maybe he is doing the rounds and there will others joining us.'

They climbed into the bus. It was basic, but comfortable. Lennardt and the driver chatted and laughed. This made Andy nervous.

They headed out of town and they were soon slipping and sliding down a wiggly lane in the sticks. A small forest emerged and disappeared. The gentle snow fall was getting more blizzard-like, but this didn't seem to phase the driver at all. Dave rubbed his hands annoyingly.

'We're in for a treat here,' he boasted. 'It's probably one of those uncensored places at a secret location on some farm somewhere.'

Andy just gestured in agreement. All he knew was they had been driving for forty minutes now and they were in the middle of nowhere.

The minibus bounced off the high drifts of snow and spun as it climbed the inclines and slid precariously as they rounded each corner. Dave could hardly contain his excitement.

'Look Andy,' he said pointing to the first lights they had seen in nearly thirty minutes. 'Not long now buddy.'

Andy managed a fake smile. They lurched up a stone driveway. The silhouette of a huge mansion was just visible as they drew closer.

*Limoncello – Perry A. Simpson*

'See, I was right.'

Andy wasn't convinced. The driver screeched to a holt in the middle if a stone courtyard. In his excitement Dave attempted to leap out of the minibus, but his legs had gone to sleep and he ended up in a crumpled heap in the deep snow. Everybody laughed. Dave was not amused.

The driver disappeared while the others stood in silence. Snow still dusting the ground around them.

'So, Dave have you worked out what is the Swedish surprise?'

For the first time all evening Dave was not so confident.

'Andy, are you glad that you came for the Swedish surprise, instead of staying the night with that nice old lady?'

Andy said nothing. The driver appeared again with a set of keys and led across the snowy courtyard to a huge Dutch barn.

'Here we go,' Dave uttered.

The doors were swung open and they all walked in. It was pitch black and completely silent. Suddenly, the lights came on and in front was a huge black stallion and small pony. Lennardt started to laugh, handing Dave and Andy half a stale loaf of bread each.

Dave and Andy looked at each other.

Andy could hold it in no longer and collapsed on the floor laughing. He had been warned about the Swedish sense of humour, but he had to admit the expression on Dave's face at that precise moment was priceless.

*Limoncello – Perry A. Simpson*

## *Desperate*

The cups and saucers rattled as Ethel struggled through the dense array of tables and chairs as she made her way to Beryl and Janet, sat at a table by the window for their usual Thursday morning tea at the Cobbler's Tea Room. She was the younger looking one of the three, with fewer grey hairs and a fairer skin complexion.

'Is Emily joining us today?' Beryl asked.

'No, she's in court today,' replied Janet.

'What for this time?' inquired Ethel.

She was doing her usual mothering thing, pouring the tea and placing each cup and saucer with the utmost precision.

'Well, she's up for dangerous driving, driving with undue care attention, and some other things. It's a long list. You know what she's like? Never does anything by half.'

Ethel sighed and sat down.

∽∾∾

'That sounds a bit serious. What did she do this time? Drive the get away car for a bank robbery?' Beryl laughed.

Janet glanced across at Beryl disapprovingly.

'Actually, it was for numerous offences while speeding.'

Beryl and Ethel both look across at Janet.

'Go on. I can see your itching to tell us,' Ethel scoffed.

'Well she was going a little bit fast on the M1.'

'How fast?' Beryl interrupted.

'Well, her top speed was 160 miles an hour when she wasn't swerving in and out of the cars.'

Ethel almost choked. Tea sprayed from her mouth.

Janet now had Beryl's and Ethel's full attention.

'She was original clocked doing 100 miles per hour by a stationary traffic cop in an unmarked patrol car.'

Janet sat back in the chair.

'They followed her for about 5 miles.'

Ethel's mouth was locked in the open position. Beryl was slowly shaking her head.

'Then, they put the siren on and attempted to get her to pull over onto the hard shoulder.'

'She didn't pull over?' Beryl interrupted.

Janet glanced across at Beryl with another disapproving expression.

'Naturally, she started to weave in and out between the cars, changing lanes. Well, that's what I heard.'

'What happened next?' Ethel asked.

'The police thought that it was a couple of joy riders and called for back-up.'

'No!' Beryl's soggy biscuit dropped into her tea.

'So, now with one cop car and a helicopter in hot pursuit, Emily was still happily weaving in and out like some madly possessed joy rider.'

'I didn't think a Nissan Micro could go that fast,' Ethel interrupted.

'Well, that's just it. It had been modified by that youngster she bought it from. It confused the police as well. They couldn't keep up with her. They eventually lost sight of her.' Janet paused. 'If it hadn't been for the helicopter she would have got clean away!' she burst out laughing.

Ethel and Beryl were still processing the information.

'I daren't ask what happened next,' exclaimed Beryl, leaning back in her chair.

*Limoncello – Perry A. Simpson*

'The police decided that it was too dangerous to continue with a high speed pursuit with all the traffic. The helicopter continued to follow her down the motorway.'

'So, Emily slowed down?' Ethel asked.

'No. At this time she was topping 160 miles an hour.'

'How long did this gone on for?' Beryl asked.

'Well, the helicopter was getting low on fuel. So, police decided to stop all the traffic coming up behind and close the motorway ahead.'

'No!'

'My good God,' Ethel gasped.

Janet nodded her head slowly. There was a pause as all three took a large gulp from their cups. They moved in closer together, leaning in for the conclusion.

'Then.' Janet paused and raised her eye brows. 'They set up a diversion to take off the remaining cars at one of the junctions ahead.'

'I need more tea,' Ethel announced. 'More tea ladies?' Janet and Beryl nodded. She got up and waded back through the tables and chairs.

The icy rain scratched at the window. The steam crept slowing down the window.

'Well, Emily never ceases to amaze me,' Beryl announced. 'Poor old Bernard must being turning in his grave.'

'Yes, he was a very good man. Totally devoted to Emily. Heaven knows why, she's never been all there."

Ethel returned with very large red pot of tea.

'Here we are ladies. This should keep us going a while.'

Her frail hand shook as she topped up the cups.

Janet continued the tale.

'So the trap was set and the cars were being slowed down by two patrol cars. Emily was now trapped in the pack of cars and all was going to plan.'

'There's a but' coming here I can tell,' Beryl rudely interrupted.

*Limoncello – Perry A. Simpson*

Ethel and Janet both scowled at Beryl.

'Emily spotted a the slip road for the service station and swerved across two lanes of cars, onto the hard shoulder and made a dash for it. The police had anticipated the possibility of this a set a stinger trap and blocked the slip road.

'The stinger is one of those spiky thing that punctures the car tyres Ethel,' interrupted Beryl.

They both looked at Janet.

'Anyway, Emily shot up the slip road, saw the road block and swerved the car up the grass verge past the stinger and the cops, and then ....'

Janet could contain herself no longer and started to laugh. The harder she tried to continue the story, the more she laughed. Much to the annoyance of Beryl and Ethel.

'Well,' Ethel snapped.

※

Janet tried to recompose herself. Tears rolled down her cheeks.

'She drove all the way to the service building and parked the car in a disabled parking space, jumped out ...' she started to laugh again.

Beryl was biting her bottom lip and Ethel grimaced.

'She flung the door open, leapt out of the car and legged it into the service station.'

Janet collapsed into another fit of laughter, tears pouring down her face.

Beryl and Ethel threw their arms in the air.

'Police cars swarmed into the car park and surrounded her car. They could see what they thought was someone in the passenger seat.'

She paused to compose herself once more.

'They moved with tasers at the ready and when they got no response fired a taser into the through the open car door.'

*Limoncello – Perry A. Simpson*

Janet started to laugh again. Wiped her eyes, sobbing now as she continued.

'Still nothing.'

'Who was in the car?' Ethel asked.

This set Janet off again. Tears began to pour down her face and she started to stutter as she spoke.

'Emily strolls out... reaches her car completely oblivious,' Janet sobbed. 'She looks inside the car and turned to the armed police and asks "what the fuck have you done to my manikin. Look, you've ruined her dress.'

All three ladies burst out laughing.

Still sobbing Janet continued.When the officer asked, what was so urgent that she had to drive so fast and recklessly?'

Tears rolled down her cheeks. Beryl and Ethel threw the arms in the air.

She replied, 'I was desperate for a piss of course.'

*Limoncello – Perry A. Simpson*

# *Switching Places*

DCI Chance looked around the scene of the crime. To his left there was an overturned chair and ornaments scattered across the floor in a straight line. He imagined the victim fighting for her life, grasping for anything that she could use to hit her assailant with. It was futile, he attacked her from behind. He was much stronger than her, and knew what he was doing, he concluded. He glanced around the crime scene once more just to be sure he hadn't overlooked anything. He instinctively knew that something didn't feel right at all. One victim in here and a second victim next door. Now, that's the first piece of the puzzle that doesn't fit this type of crime, he surmised.

⁓✧⁓

'What do you have for me Malcolm?,' he asked.

Malcolm Ward, detective sergeant, was tall, slim in build with short cropped hair and a bleak complexion.

'Well sir, victim number one is Martha McCarthy, aged 42. She was strangled in here. There appears to have been a bit of a struggle as you can see.'

'She's the wife of the killer?'

'Yes sir. The second victim is Mr. Jeremy Clarke, aged 36, solicitor, divorced and lived alone. He was killed next door in his own home.'

He paused to turn to the next page in his little black note book.

'Mr. Clarke was brutally beaten to death.'

'It would have more convenient if they were both found half naked, in bed or at least killed together in the same place,' Chance said.

'It seems a clear case of a crime of passion. He finds out that his wife is having an affair with a younger man who happens to live next door. He just snaps, kills his wife then pops round next door to terminate the lover.'

'Do we know who he killed first?' Chance asked.

'Well actually we don't. We won't know until the autopsy results come in Sir.'

'It all looks too convenient, don't you think Malcolm?'

'Well, it isn't the first time Sir.'

'No?'

The Sergeant leafed through his little book.

'Well, according to the house-to-house, this is not the first time Donald McCarthy has been involved in an incident involving his wife.'

'I trust that you are already looking into that?'

'Yes Sir. I am waiting for a call back from records.'

'Good. Let's go and look at the second victim, Mr. ?'

'Mr. Clarke, Sir.'

They retraced their steps over the aluminium boards, out the red front door, walked across the thin strip of patchy grass and entered the adjacent door.

∽✼∾

Chance noted that this crime scene was much messier. The attack was more frenzied. Jeremy Clarke wasn't a very big man and it seemed likely that he was also hit from behind, over powering him so that Donald McCarthy could finish him off. Chance also noted the amount of overkill.

'Where is McCarthy now?'

'Down the station Sir.'

*Limoncello – Perry A. Simpson*

'We do not really have anything to link the two victims. We need to find evidence that they were having an affair.'

Chance had an uneasy feeling about this case.

'Ward, can you arrange for copies of SMS transcripts and calls from their mobiles? Oh, and find out if they exchanged any emails.'

Ward nodded, as he reached for his ringing phone. He frowned, then thanked the caller, turning back to Chance. 'Sir, it would appear that Donald McCarthy is already in prison serving a sentence for attempting to kill his wife.'

'Then who do we had in custody back at the station?'

Chance had to admit that this was an unexpected twist.

---

Chance stood in silence with his back pressed against the wall in the dimly lit interview room. Slumped over the heavy steel table, handcuffed to the rail, the real Donald McCarthy stared, angrily into the distance.

'For the tape, please state your name,' Ward instructed

McCarthy said nothing.

Chance slammed the folder on the table. 'Who have we got banged up in Wandsworth for attempting to strangle your wife?'

McCarthy didn't stir.

'According to our DNA records you should be banged up.'

Again, McCarthy refused to acknowledge Chance.

'Maybe we should ask your mother to come down to the station to identify you.

'You leave her out of this, do you hear?'

McCarthy thumped the desk with his badly bruised fists.

'Is it Ronald, your twin brother?'

McCarthy looked up at Chance, eyes cold, lost, disconnected and nodded.

*Limoncello – Perry A. Simpson*

Chance sat down opposite him, opened the folder and looked McCarthy in the eye.

'In your own time.'

'Ronald and I are twins, but he was always the stronger. He always took the blame for everything, even when it wasn't him that was in the wrong.'

Chance had already worked out the switching of places by his overprotective brother Ronald.

'What about your father.'

'Never knew him. Upped and left before we was even born.'

'Tell me about the murders Donald. Why did you kill your wife and your neighbour.'

Donald eyes grew cold and harsh.

'They were having an affair.'

'How did you find out about the affair?'

Chance was intrigued by this particular point as he had the SMS transcripts in his hand.

'He sent me a text. Not only was he shagging my wife, he felt he had to rub my nose in it.'

Donald's clenched his fists tightly, head swaying back forth.

'It's OK Donald, just take your time.' Chance said reassuringly.

There was a long pause while Donald calmed down. Chance glanced through the transcripts.

'Problem is Donald we cannot find any link between your wife and Mr. Clarke. No SMS exchange. No emails. No secret letters. No entries in your wife's diary. In fact nothing.'

Donald glanced up at Chance, 'The smart arse sent me a bloody SMS, I tell you.'

'What did the SMS say Donald?'

'Oh, I cannot remember. It was something about helping himself to my wife.'

*Limoncello – Perry A. Simpson*

The door opened and a young female officer handed sergeant Ward some sheets of paper. Chance got up and left the room.

Chance returned to the interview room and Ward announced that DCI Chance had returned to the interview for the tape.

'Donald, I have here the transcript of the SMS that Mr. Clarke sent to your mobile phone. We have tallied the times that the SMS was sent to the times they were received and read on your iPhone.

Donald looked up at Chance and nodded for him to go on.

'The transcript reads like this:'

"Don, I'm sorry. I've been riddled with guilt for sometime now and I have to confess I have been helping myself to your wife when you're not around. I have been having problems connecting. My life has been such a mess of late and I hope you'll accept my sincerest apology. It won't happen again."

Chance placed the transcript on the table in front of Donald. He nodded gently.

Chance continued, 'You were feeling so outraged and betrayed, that you grabbed your wife's neck from behind and straggled her to death.'

Donald nodded in agreement.

'For the tape Mr. McCarthy,' sergeant in Ward insisted.

'Yes,' Donald said softly.

'Then you went next door and bludgeoned Mr. Clarke to death,' sergeant Ward said forcefully.

'Yes.' Donald McCarthy was broken.

*Limoncello – Perry A. Simpson*

Sergeant Ward commenced with the caution of Donald McCarthy for the murder of his wife and their neighbour.

'Not so fast sergeant,' Chance interrupted. 'There's more.'

Donald, the sergeant and the duty solicitor looked up at DCI Chance.

Chanced continued, 'Moments after you received that message, Mr Clarke sent another text:

"Damn, I really should deactivate predictive text!"

'What difference does that make?' Ward challenged.

Chance smiled, 'When Mr. Clarke referred to your wife Donald, he actually typed wifi, but the predictive text feature on his mobile filled it in as "wife". Your wife, Martha, was not having an affair.

*Limoncello – Perry A. Simpson*

# Aunt Marge

Amy Smith, a teacher at Lintel Blake Primary School, was contemplating what the new proposed DfE assessments would entail. For many teachers it could be the prospect of results being used by Ofsted to measure teacher performance by stealth. She had been told that the Department for Education claimed that this was all about children leaving primary school with a good standard of reading, writing and maths. Amy knew that it wasn't her teaching ability that was the root of the problem, but the crap she was expected to teach from the failing standard curriculum. Well, tomorrow the kids would have a day off from all that boring stuff. She would engage her little people in a meaningful exercise.

---

The children filed noisily in through the door and hung their coats on the multi-coloured hanger rail. The noise level slowly rose.

Amy made her way to the front of the class and raised her arm. The chattering voices slowly stopped and the room was silent.

'Today, I am going to tell you the story about "The Hare and the Tortoise".'

A tiny hand slowly rose.

'Yes, Tommy.'

'I know that story.'

'Good. Would you like to help me tell the rest of the class the story, Tommy?'

Tommy nodded. His little round face lit up.

'How does the story start?'

Tommy shuffled his weight on the chair.

'Once upon a time, there was a hare who went to a pond to have drink. As he drank the water, he saw a slow-moving tortoise over on the path and started to make fun of him.'

He paused, thinking what came next.

'What did the tortoise do?' Amy asked the rest of the class.

Silence fell upon the room.

'The tortoise was not happy and challenged the hare for a race,' Tommy continued. 'The hare said "yes" with a big smile.'

A couple of children laughed and the noise level rose again.

'And the next morning?' Amy asked.

This quietened the class.

'They both met at the starting point and the race began. Soon the hare went far ahead of the tortoise. When the hare reached half way he got bored as the tortoise was quite far behind.'

'What did the hare do?'

'He took a rest and began eating fresh green grass. He felt tired so he had a sleep in the shade of a bush.'

'Good Tommy, keep going.'

Amy was impressed with him and her little experiment.

Tommy sat swinging his legs, 'The tortoise moved along at his slow pace and overtook the sleeping hare. He reached the finish and won the race.'

He paused, smiled and looked up at Amy.

'Go on Tommy.'

'When the hare woke up, it was fairly late. He was worried that the tortoise might have passed by him as he

*Limoncello – Perry A. Simpson*

slept. So he ran at a really fast speed until he reached the finish post, but the tortoise was already there. The tortoise was the winner of the race – the end!'

Tommy sat down.

The rest of the class clapped and the chattering of children filled the air.

'Thank you Tommy for sharing that story with the class.'

Tommy blushed.

'So, what does this story teach us?'

The little faces just looked at Amy waiting for the answer.

'This story teaches us that, one who moves steadily though slow, is never a loser. That's why we say, "Slow and steady, wins the race. We call this a "moral" story as it teaches us something.'

Some of the children began to fidget.

'Now, what I would like you to do is ask your mums, dads, grandmas, granddads or aunties for a moral story to share with the class at our next lesson.'

A little hand slowly rose in the middle of the room.

'Yes, Shaun?'

'Miss, do I have to visit all of my aunties and uncles?'

'No, not all of them, no of course not,' she laughed.

'Good, I seem to have hundreds of em!'

A little girl slowly raised her hand.

It was Katie, a bright, quiet little girl from a very troubled and unstable background. A regular absentee. She lived alone with her father. A really nice man, who seemed to work all hours to make ends meet. Constantly fighting off the social workers, as she recalled.

'Katie, come and talk to me after the class.'

Katie stood up slowly. Her hair was tied up in uneven pony tails at each side of her head. She had matching scuffs on her knees and the tips of her shoes, offsetting her red school tie around her neck. When she smiled an air of confidence filled the room.

*Limoncello – Perry A. Simpson*

'I have a story miss.'

Amy was taken aback. When Katie did attend school she was normally very withdrawn, quiet, and there in body, but not in spirit. This was a quite unexpected development, proving her point about the lack of creativity in the curriculum. She smiled in acknowledgment.

'Katie, the stage is yours. We would all love to hear your story, wouldn't we everyone?'

There was a resounding yes.

'This story is about my Aunt Marge,' she announced, her voice clear, but soft.

'Aunt Marge was in the Marines and was on a special mission to the Falkland Islands.'

This was met with a big "wow" from the now captive audience. Amy raised a smile.

'Anyway, something went wrong and the helicopter she was flying in crashed in the sea.'

'What went wrong?' asked Tommy.

'Ah, some idiots fucked up back at base. Gave them the wrong co-ordinates or something.'

There was a loud gasp.

'Katie, we do not use that sort of language in class,' Amy said raising a disapproving finger.

'Sorry miss.'

'Apology accepted, please continue.'

'Aunt Marge swam to shore and found herself alone behind enemy lines.'

There was another gasp.

'What did she do?' Tommy interrupted.

'She assessed the situation and it was not good. She was surrounded by a hundred enemy troops. All she had was a bottle of Jameson's, a machine gun, and a big knife.'

Katie paused, turned and looked at all her classmates.

She had captured the attention of the whole class and Katie started to mime each action.

*Limoncello – Perry A. Simpson*

'She drank the whiskey to calm her nerves.'

Katie simulated the action of guzzling down the whiskey, pretending to smash the bottle on the ground. Then, she leapt around the room pretending she had a machine gun.

'She charged in like a mad idiot, shooting 70 enemy troops, until she ran out of bullets.'

She pretended to casually throw the gun to one side, took out a knife and crept slowly around the class.

'It was chaos, so she crept around like a panther leaping out and killing 20 more with her big knife, until her knife broke.'

Her eyes were now fierce and menacing.

'She killed the last ten with her bare hands, snapping theirs necks one-by-one.'

Katie turned and walked back to the front of the class.

'Good grief, Katie, is that story actually true?'

'Yes, my dad says it is and he wouldn't dare tell a lie about Aunt Marge.'

Amy knew she would regret asking, 'So what did your dad tell you was the moral of this story?'

'Don't fuck with Aunt Marge when she's been drinking.'

## *Flowers*

Neil Lambert sat quietly on a tired wooden bench as he watched a small wren picking through the dried leaves surrounding the headstones. It's busy movements had temporarily distracted him from his thoughts. It had been five years now and he could no longer be consumed with the guilt of that fateful day. Sat next to him was a man, smartly dressed in a navy blue suit, highly polished shoes, clean shaven, hair neatly combed to one side. He too, was engrossed in his thoughts.

'Have you ever reached a point in your life where you feel that the only way out of situation is to just end it?' Neil asked the stranger.

This brought the stranger back to reality, 'Yes, I just came back.'

Neil Lambert placed his hands on his knees, his badly bitten finger nails in clear view. He tapped the heels of his shoes on the floor beneath the bench.

―⁂―

The stranger spoke softly, 'Do you want to talk about it?'

Neil Lambert placed his hands back in his pockets and started to play with the contents.

'Five years ago, I did something bad.'

'Bad enough to commit suicide?'

The stranger noticed the bunch of flowers on the bench set down beside him.

'Well yes, it seemed to be the only way.'

'It's a bit selfish if you ask me. You'll hurt all the people close to you. Trust me I know, it is not the answer.'

Neil Lambert shifted his balance on the bench. Feet twitching.

'Five years ago, I was involved in a car accident' he paused. 'A little boy died and it was my fault.'

'People die everyday, even children. Hardly justifies taking your own life.'

Neil Lambert began to jingle the change in his pocket.

'It was Friday 20th June 2008. It was my 10th work anniversary with my firm. We sat at the breakfast table together as a family. I did not know that it would be the last.' Tiny beads of sweat formed on his brow.

The stranger remained motionless and said nothing.

'I arrived at work in time for my morning coffee before I started my hectic day. I noticed that everyone was staring at me. When I got to my desk, there was a small brown envelope placed in the centre. I knew before I even opened it what it was. Ten bloody years I'd given to that firm. They didn't even have the decency to hand it to me personally.'

'A redundancy notice.'

'Yes, the company has been experiencing difficulties in it's first quarter and we regret to inform that your service ...'

'What did you do?'

'I was in shock for several minutes, then I noticed all the other empty spaces, where a happy team of workers once sat. I took a flip chart pen out from my drawer and wrote "Valéte!" in huge letters across embedded vinyl pad on the desk.'

'Meaning?'

'Good bye, in Latin. I mentally prepared myself for when I arrived home. My wife had just booked the summer holiday in Miami. To really rub salt into my wounds, when I did eventually get home, I found my wife in bed with my best friend, Terrence.'

Neil Lambert paused, fists clenched.

'Don't tell, you whacked him?'

'No, I just stormed out again and headed for the nearest pub.'

'The Compass?'

Neil Lambert nodded as he was rocked back and forth on the bench, reliving every moment as if it had just happened. He started to cry.

The stranger just sat quietly allowing Neil Lambert to calm himself.

'Drunk as a skunk, I climbed into my car and swerved off. Amazingly, I found myself back in control, until ...' He started to sob. He thumped the bench with both fists. 'Someone ran out in front of me. I'll never forget that dull thud as a head smashed against the windscreen. The car skidded until it hit the kerb. I sat there frozen in the seat. My hands were still locked to the wheel – I couldn't let go.'

The stranger just sat there expressionless, motionless, and looking into the distance. To interrupt Neil Lambert's flow now would be a mistake, thought the stranger.

'Eventually, I got out of the car and slowly walked around to the front of the car. There before me was a mangled little body in a pool of blood.'

He continued to sob. Wiping his eyes, he continued, 'I panicked, turned and ran. I had no idea where I was going, I just kept running. When I stopped, I was sober. In less than a day my whole world had collapsed.'

'What do you plan to do?'

Neil Lambert seemed to take some time to process the question. He gazed down at the flowers, suddenly remembering, 'I plan to place some flowers on his grave and then, I may as well kill myself.'

'What will that solve?'

'What the fuck has that got to do with you? He snapped.

*Limoncello – Perry A. Simpson*

Jumping to his feet, Neil Lambert snatched the flowers and stomped off in an easterly direction into the graveyard.

※

Neil Lambert walked around aimlessly, looking for the headstone of the little boy he had killed that fateful night. He was getting tired of reading the newish headstones and was about to give up, when, he saw his own parents standing beside a grave. He hid behind a tree and watched as his mum sobbed into a tissue. His father guided her away from the grave and they slowly walked towards the west gate. Neil was stunned. He hadn't contacted anyone since that night, not even his parents.

That must be the little boys grave, he thought. Plucking up courage, he came out from behind the tree and walked down to the grave. He looked at the headstone and upon reading it, fell to his knees.

It read, "In loving memory of Neil James Lambert died Friday 20th June 2008."

The stranger re-appeared and handed him a card and spoke softly, 'If you change your mind, contact me and tell me what happened that night.' He turned and walked gently towards the west gate.

Neil turned the card over and read the details on the card, "DCI Chance, Metropolitan Police."

# Movie Night

'My beer, your wine, the crisps and not forgetting the chocolates,' William announced as Anne swept into the room, struggling to contain her excitement.

William and Anne Wyatt were about to settle down to watch a horror movie. Anne enjoys being scared out of her wits.

'It's fun,' she once told William.

He on the other hand, simply liked being distracted from his mundane life, vicariously sticking his finger up at social norms, and enjoying that voyeuristic glimpse of the horrific from the safety of his own home. Anne grabbed a cushion and the remote stood while William turned off the lights and joined Anne on the sofa. They shuffled in close and Anne started the movie.

⁂

The still darkness in the room was soon disturbed by the erratic bursts of light from the television as the story started to unfold. It was completely dark. Silent. Anne could hear her heart slowly pumping. She clutched the cushion tightly and slowly raised it until she was peeking over the top of it.

There was a sudden burst of light from the television followed by a chilling scream, then a slow ripping sound as a curtain slowly popped the clips from the rail. Crash! The curtain rail couldn't take the strain any more and came crashing down. Anne buried her head into the cushion. The light was poor, she couldn't see much, but still she was too scared to look.

All was silent. The room went dark. The dragging sound broke the silence. The victim was being dragged across the floor.

William looked round towards the neighbours wall. He was convinced that the sound had actually come from there and not from the television set. The dragging sound ended with a dull thud as the feet fell back to the floor. William sat upright and looked across at the neighbours' wall.

Anne came out from behind her cushion, 'what's up with you?'

William waved his right hand to silence Anne while he listened.

Groaning noises could be heard. Anne focused on the TV set from the safety of her cushion. William's attention was still transfixed on the neighbours' wall.

A grunting sound was shortly followed by a heavy fall softened by the springiness of the mattress. It went dark again. Then deathly silence, broken by an evil laugh. A loud scream tore through the air, filling the room. Anne bit the cushion. William stood up.

The terrifying scream was replaced with a muffled moaning sound.

Another sudden burst of light was followed by a violent ripping sound as the victims clothes were torn from her body. A struggle followed. The light was poor, but Anne could just make out the image of the victim was being handcuffed to the bed.

'Where are you going! William?'

William was walking towards the wall that separated them from their neighbours. He was listening intently.

'For a moment then, I could swear that the noises were coming from next door.'

*Limoncello – Perry A. Simpson*

'Come and sit back down. It's just this new surround sound system.'

William shrugged his shoulders and rejoined Anne on the sofa.

The groans from the victim weakened. Her attacker remained in the cover of darkness. A flash of light from the window drew a reflection from a large, wide bladed knife.

Anne gasped.

William was still distracted. His attention now focused on the passing cars outside. They seemed to sound louder, he thought.

The tension began to rise slowly with the music. Anne braced herself for another frightening twist.

There was an eruption of violence, crashing, objects falling, fragile glass and pottery smashing across the floor. It seemed to go on for ages. Anne couldn't take eyes off the dark figure creating chaos in the rooms while the victim awaited her fate.

William stood up once more. He walked slowly back and forth.

'What's gotten into you tonight?' Anne snapped.

'I'm not convinced that this is coming from the surround system Anne.'

'Come and sit back down. You're spoiling the atmosphere.'

William sighed, surrendered and returned to Anne's side.

A passing light through the window provided another brief glimpse of the knife. This time raised high, ready to strike its victim.

Anne gasped, raising the cushion.

A really agonisingly loud scream ripped across the room, followed by an extremely loud bang. Anne screamed, burying her face into the cushion.

William jumped and cursed Anne's over-reaction.

*Limoncello – Perry A. Simpson*

It went dark. All was Silent. Anne reached for her wine. William reached for his beer. The cold silence was interrupted by a slow dripping sound in the darkness.

'Blood,' Anne whispered.

William looked up, trying to pinpoint the source of the sounds which appeared to be above him.

A low murmur came from the victim, growing longer and louder.

'She's still alive,' Anne shouted.

'Can't be,' William argued.

He hadn't let on, but he had already seen the movie.

'See, there it is again.'

William leapt to his feet and stomped over to the TV set. He turned the sound volume down.

They both looked at one another as the groaning continued.

William turned the sound back up just to confirm. He muted the sound altogether.

'See, I knew I wasn't hearing things. Surround sound my arse,' he laughed. 'Those idiots next door are at it again. Always creating, arguing, making a noise. Well, I've just had enough of it.'

'What are you going to do?' Anne asked.

'I'm going to phone the police – they can deal with it. There's got to be some law against it,' he stuttered.

He picked up the phone and made a call to the police.

༺∞༻

The police arrived at the scene within ten minutes of the call.

'Mr Wyatt?'

'Yes.'

'I am PC Mattock and this is WPC Granger. You called the emergency services regarding a disturbance.'

'Yes, that's correct. It's our neighbours – there was a lot of crashing, banging and strange noises. All we can hear now is a groaning noise.'

'Something's happened officer,' Anne butted in.

'Where did you hear these noises?'

'From our living room. We were watching a movie and we could hear the noises above the TV.'

'Can you still here the noises?'

'Well, just a groaning noise.'

'Can we take a look?'

The young stocky officer, accompanied by a young WPC followed the Wyatts into the living room. Both PC were wearing flat jackets with an array of equipment on a belt around their waists. They listened.

'Well, it appears to be coming from above us.'

'That's ridiculous, that's our bedroom.'

'Can we take a look sir.'

'Yes, yes, be my guest.'

They slowly climbed the stairs. The groaning noise grew louder as they closed in on the Wyatt's bedroom. Both officers stopped at the closed bedroom.

'This is the police.'

They waited several seconds. No response.

'This is the police. We are entering the room.'

He slowly turned the handle and pushed the door ajar. It was dark and a sudden breeze hit them. PC Mattock reached for the light switch.

WPC Granger joined him at the entrance. They were greeted with a scene of what appeared to be complete carnage. The curtains and rail were on the floor, clips and rings scattered everywhere. The window was open. The book case had collapsed, books scattered haphazardly. The wardrobe was facedown, a long way off from its correct location.

*Limoncello – Perry A. Simpson*

On the bed was a middle aged women dressed as little Red Riding Hood – red cape, matching dress and shoes. She was tied to the bed posts and gagged. She was barely conscious. WPC Granger removed the gag. Little Red Riding Hood gasped and pointed to the wardrobe.

PC Mattock approached with caution. Together, the officers rolled the wardrobe onto its side. The WPC took out her taser, pointing it at the door. PC Mattock slowly turned the key.

The door burst open and a wolf fell out. They all jumped. Upon closer examination, they could see it was a man dressed as a wolf.

William and Anne Wyatt were in a state of shock.

'Do you know these people?'

'Yes, the perverts from next door,' Anne laughed.

*Limoncello – Perry A. Simpson*

## Sexual Exhaustion

Karen Greenwood smiled as she retrieved another empty glass. She assumed that Doug Adams, a regular, didn't need asking if he needed a refill. Doug liked this place. Unlike most pubs, "Ye Olde Cheshire Cheese" was not part of any of these big chains, there were no games machines, pool table or Sky Sports to spoil the ambience. This was a pub where Doug could simply enjoy a quiet drink in relaxed surroundings with it's cosy atmosphere.

Tonight was different. Two strangers had entered the usually quiet Tuesday night crowd. He watched them closely. One of these lads did seem familiar to Doug, but he couldn't quite place where from. He quickly concluded that the other one was a ponce. Doug was in a really good mood until these two idiots had walked in.

꘏

Ian York and David Meade struggled onto the old wooden high bar chairs. Karen pulled two pints of Chatsworth Gold and placed them on the drip mat in front of the weary lads, 'You two look like you need a drink.'

'You ain't kidding,' Ian said clutching the pint glass.

Dave who was the calmer of the two, took his glass, winked at the tall, leggy brunette. 'Thank you my love.'

'Yorkie, I have to say you looked completely shagged out,' Dave laughed out loudly.

'Dave, I am exhausted.'

'Olga?'

'Yes, Olga the non-stop sex machine. I do not how much more of this I can take.'

Ian took another large gulp and shook his head.

'It could be worse.'

'How could it?'

'At least with Olga it's not kinky stuff.'

'Samantha?'

'Yes,' Dave sighed.

'What is it now? Another bondage nightmare?'

Dave was not amused. He took a larger slurp from his glass. 'She wants us to write down ten sexual fantasies.'

'Really?'

'Yes. It wouldn't be so bad if I could actually think of ten.'

Ian started to laugh, 'Well?'

'Well what?'

'How many have you got?'

Dave began to blush a little, 'Five.'

'Five! Your girlfriend offers you your ten dream sexual fantasies and you can only come up with five!'

'Oh, I bet you have ten written up and rehearsed? Yet, here you are saying that you cannot cope with marathon Olga.'

That little outburst from Dave prompted Ian to order another round of drinks, which the ever efficient Karen delivered.

'So what are you going to do about your list?'

'Get creative, I guess. OK, smart arse, let's hear yours then,' Dave demanded.

'Well, let's explore the options: top of my list would be joining the mile high club with a complete stranger, then a threesome. Girl-on-girl is also high on my list. Sex in a moving car, on a busy public beach, cleavage sex, dominatrix, exhibitionism, bit of bondage, role play would also be popular choices.

*Limoncello – Perry A. Simpson*

'Something tells me you have already fulfilled some of these.'

'What are you going to do about marathon Olga?'

'I need to wangle a couple of nights off the sex.'

⁓⁕⁓

They were interrupted by the chuckles from a few seats up. Ian and Dave glanced over at Doug Adams slumped over the bar.

Dave looked back at Yorkie, 'That's shouldn't be too difficult. A couple of nights out with the lads should do the trick.'

'I'm not so sure Dave – she's on fire at the moment and I think that it is of my own doing.'

'How do you mean?'

'When we first met the sex was five or six times a week. You know? Then, after about six weeks, it was only a drunken shag on a Friday night out. Well, I read an article that when your partner is less interested than you, then you should focus your attention on the friendship as most women are wired that way.'

'So, how does that work then?' Dave mused.

'Well, the article went on to say that you should show your affection with random acts of kindness.'

'Like what?' He huffed.

'Doing more things as a couple, like going shopping, buying her small gifts, calling her at the office to tell how much I loved her, give a single red rose with her cup of tea in the morning.'

'Your having me on?'

'No, straight up. She came home from work one evening just wearing a full length coat and knee length boots and nothing else. Now ...'

'Sounds like you pressed an accelerate button.' Dave laughed.

*Limoncello – Perry A. Simpson*

'Yes, now when we are together, it's three or four times a night – Minimum.'

'I have to say, Yorkie, you have a way with the girls, but that little Russian number has got you tied up.'

'No, that's planned for Thursday.'

'Yorkie me old mate, this is getting serious. Sure you don't need to include a friend in one of your sessions.'

'That'll wouldn't slow her down.'

'No, but it would give you a chance to catch your breath. Dave laughed, slopping some of his beer on the bar top.

'Dave, I really need to find a way to turn the heat down, slow things down to moderate.'

'Yorkie, this is not a cooker you're taking about her. This is a ticking Russian Nymphomaniac.'

'Don't, it's some sort of clock thing tonight.'

⁓∞⁓

Doug began to chuckle once more.

This really annoyed Dave.

'What's so funny old man?' he snapped.

'You youngsters haven't a clue when comes to understanding members of the opposite sex.'

'You're an expert on the subject, I suppose?'

'Well, let's say, I've had a few more years practise.'

Ian looked at Dave, 'There's always one?'

'Meaning?' Doug sneered.

'There's always a know it all.'

'Well, I know the answer to your friends little problem.'

'Can't wait for this,' Dave laughed. 'Go on then, what would you do, if you were in his position?'

A huge grin separated Doug's chin from the rest of his face, 'Simple, just marry her. Trust me, once your married your sex life will be reduced to an occasional shag.'

'Huh, you speak for yourself,' Ian challenged.

*Limoncello – Perry A. Simpson*

'It's not your cock she after. That's just a means of to get what she really wants.'

Ian shook his head, '... and that is?'

'Life's umbrella.'

'This guys barking ...,' Dave laughs.

'Roof over her head, family, security. When she has all that she doesn't need to fuck your brains out any more,' Doug proudly announced.

'Olga might not be like that at all.'

'Oh, she will be.'

'How would you know?'

'Olga is just like her mother. Twenty five years ago, I sat in this very bar with a similar predicament as you with Olga's mother.'

Ian could feel a radiant glow spread across his cheeks. Dave joined Doug in laughter.

*Limoncello – Perry A. Simpson*

## *Forties Night*

A forties night did sound appealing, but not with the Plummer's, pondered Thomas. Thomas Palmer was fine with the weekend breaks with Steve Plummer, but an evening out with the wives was straying into uncharted waters. Thomas tried to imagine Steve Plummer with too many drinks at a forties night fancy dress dance.

He glanced out into the moonlit garden to distract his thoughts. Thomas knew that his wife, Sandra, was really looking forward to the whole forties thing and he therefore felt obligated.

Thomas's social gatherings usually involved wearing a smart tuxedo and drinking very expensive champagne. Chicken in a basket supper with endless supply of beer didn't quite have the same appeal

'What are you going as?' probed Thomas.
'Well, that would spoil the surprise,' Sandra teased.
'Oh, please don't do this to me Sandra.'
'You'll have to wait till tonight,' Sandra smiled.

～⁂～

Thomas was too preoccupied to work. Steve had been badgering him all day and trying to work proved to be futile. He snatched his jacket from the hanger and headed for home.

His journey home was a blur.

'Had a good day at office darling?'

'No, not really. Steve hassled me all day about this forties night.'

'Likewise. Gillian called twice'

'What about for heavens sake?'

'You know, the usual, but I am sure she was trying to find out about outfits for tonight.'

'Still think this was a good idea of yours?'

'Yes, it will be fun.'

Thomas sighed.

'I went to see your mother today. She sorted us out with a couple of outfits for this evening.'

'You are kidding?'

'You will be escorting me as an official Naval Officer in dinner dress.'

Thomas glanced over to where Sandra pointed.

'Your father's apparently.'

Thomas chuckled nervously.

'You didn't tell me your father was an officer in the Royal Navy.'

Thomas just nodded. He wasn't comfortable with the idea of wearing his father's clothes.

'What are you going to be wearing?'

Sandra winked at him and ran off upstairs excitedly and reappeared several minutes later wearing a beautiful cream evening dress.

Thomas was speechless.

'I've even pre-booked our taxi for seven thirty. So, we do not have too much time.'

---

Thomas stood in front of the a steamed up mirror wrestling with his black bow tie.

'Come here,' Sandra said taking charge, resulting in a perfect bow.

*Limoncello – Perry A. Simpson*

'Where did you learn to do that?'

'My mother taught me as a child. She would often say that one day you might meet an officer.' She chuckled.

―⁂―

The moonlight sky placed a spotlight on the gleaming black car as it drew up outside their front door. An elderly gentlemen got out and gracefully opened the doors, Sandra's first, followed by Thomas. The interior of the car was immaculately clean with a very distinctive smell of musty leather. They were both pleasantly surprised as they were usually greeted with a gorilla-like grunt from some ill-mannered driver wearing a dirty old baseball cap.

The driver said nothing.

'It's a bit chilly in here,' Sandra whispered, feeling a little uneasy.

Thomas said nothing. He began to suspect this could, somehow, be some practical joke of Steve's making.

―⁂―

The car suddenly lurched onto a stony driveway and pulled up at a large stoop of wonderful stoned washed building. The "Lasky's" spanned across the large oak doors.

They both watched as the car faded into the darkness.

Sandra began to feel very oppressed and slightly sick, as if she was slipping into a dream. She stumbled a couple a steps from the top.

'Are you all right darling?' Thomas asked.

'Yes. I am fine.'

'Yes, I could murder a G&T after our little taxi ride.'

'I think I could get used to being chauffeured around,' Sandra teased.

Thomas saw no sign of the Plummers, but he was expecting them to leap out on them at any moment.

*Limoncello – Perry A. Simpson*

They were ushered into the main dance hall, where a waiter carrying a tray handed them a glass of champagne. They walked slowly round the large hall, tables and chairs hugged the perimeter in the walls in the haze of cigarette smoke. In the centre of the domed ceiling a chandelier shimmered gently in the rhythmic atmosphere. The dance floor was alive with wriggling bodies dancing to the live music, played by the band occupying the stage at the far end.

Sandra noticed that the young officer heading towards them had an unusual limp. As he drew closer Sandra began to feel queasy again. It was as if she was walking in her sleep and her feet were getting heavier with each step. She felt her legs starting to give way and dived towards the nearest chair. The closer she got to the chair the further away it seemed to be, until, she eventually stumbled, only to be caught by the young officer.

'Sandra, are you all right,' Thomas gasped.

He helped the young officer perch her on the edge of the chair.

A waiter offered her a glass of water and a soft, slightly moistened handkerchief.

'Thank you', she said catching her breath. She took a sip. 'What the hell is happening to me?,' she muttered.

Thomas turned to thank the young officer, but he was no longer there. They both just sat and watched as the couples waltzed around the floor.

Sandra was still feeling uncomfortable. She knew something wasn't quite right. Everything around her seemed to be real enough, but had a shallow appearance. All the colours seem bleached. She also noticed how the voices and music were diminished in tone, as in phonograph.

'It's an impressive display,' Thomas said, breaking the silence.

'What is?'

*Limoncello – Perry A. Simpson*

'The attention to detail. Look, they've even got black out screens on the windows.'

The strange sensation that had almost floored Sandra earlier had now receded and she was feeling much perkier. She noticed that the fancy dress worn by all the people was so authentic.

---

The sudden appearance of the waiter startled them.

'Your driver is waiting for you. You need to leave right away without delay.' he insisted.

Thomas helped Sandra to her feet and clutching one another they followed him swiftly to the door.

'You didn't say anything about organising a taxi to pick us up.'

'I didn't,' Sandra replied.

The crisp night air was crowned with a clear sky filled with the sparkle of distant stars. Suddenly, the sky became ablaze with flashing light. A thunderstorm brewed in the distance. A low rumble rolled across the sky towards them.

Thomas turned to the driver, 'Looks like a storm brewing.'

He didn't reply.

The car moved off swiftly. The flashing intensified, causing the driver to speed up. When they arrived at the house, the flashing had mysteriously ceased and the sky was peaceful again.

Sandra and Thomas were relieved to be home.

---

'What happened to you last night? Gillian asked.

'Well, we were there.'

'Steve and I looked everywhere for you.'

'Look, we were at the Lasky's club last night and left before the storm.'

'Lasky's?, but the venue for the forties night was the old corn exchange. It was written on the ticket.'

There was a pause while Sandra quickly rewound all the night's events, then checked the ticket.

'Lasky's club was blitzed during a heavy bombing raid, killing all the guests at a private party with the exception of two, a young naval officer and his girlfriend, who had left minutes earlier because she was not feeling so good.'

Sandra's chin dropped.

*Limoncello – Perry A. Simpson*

# *Spirit of Christmas*

It was Christmas Eve once more. The time of year that now provided Cathy with a painful reminder of how lonely she was. This would be her third year without her family to share the festivities. In fact, it was exactly three years to the day, that her dear old dad had died. She remembered it as though it was yesterday and the pain always returned during the run up to Christmas.

As a teenage girl she had convinced herself that he would live forever. This strong, well built and stocky figure of man that she adored so much was reduced to a mere skeleton from the day he threw her little brother Richard out of the house. It was one of those heat of the moment things that he regretted after the event, but Richard never did return.

Her mother said that he had died of guilt. On the night of his funeral, she too passed away peacefully in her sleep.

---

This year Cathy had turned down the usual offers from friends of the family. She had decided that Christmas was going to be different this year by spending a peaceful Christmas by herself.

Everything was organised: the turkey, the vegetables, the tree, the decorations, the Christmas cards and so on. It was Saturday and the last of the presents had been delivered. Cathy actually began to feel much more optimistic about the future.

Her fragile finger tips tapped the steering wheel. The music from the Christmas jingles from the car radio just blended in with the chorus of engines, as everyone jostled for position.

The weather had suddenly turned and a biting frost was sprung upon the people of London.

Underneath the bridge of the flyover a small group of homeless people huddled around a burning rubbish basket, a source of some warmth for the unfortunate few. Adrift from the crowd, a lonely figure sat hunched over a small sign. She couldn't quite make out the words scrawled on the crumbled piece of card. Curiosity got the better of her. She stopped the car.

"Loneliness and the . . ."

Intrigued, Cathy wound the window down to get a better look. The message board was made from the lid of cardboard box, propped up by a small empty baked bean tin.

The traffic in front of her started to move again forcing her to edge forward.

'Of course,' she muttered. 'Loneliness and the feeling of being unwanted is the most terrible poverty,' reading the words out loud. 'Mother Teresa.'

Cathy realised that she had something in common with this homeless person. She will also be sitting alone at home on Christmas Day. He would be sat there hoping to scrape enough loose change together to get a burger and a coffee from MacDonald's. It was then that the idea came to her. The remainder of the journey was a blur.

∽∾∾

Cathy poured herself a healthy measure of brandy, pulled her chair closer to the raging fake log fire and contemplated the notion of inviting this complete stranger to spend

Christmas Day with her. It was a crazy idea – potentially dangerous too, she thought. He could be anybody or anything!

Her mind went into overdrive debating the pros and cons of this wonderful, but careless gesture.

A sudden burst of sunlight through the lounge window filled the room with warmth that bathed Cathy in a radiant glow. She saw this as a sign, something she had not experienced in years. Cathy was inspired. Her heart was yearning to meet this man who had sought comfort in those well chosen words.

⁂

The turkey was cooking in the oven, the vegetables were ready, and there was no shortage of drink.

Cathy parked the car and decided to continue her search on foot. There was no turning back now.

She found him still slumped in the same spot. As she approached her heart pounded uncontrollably, alerting her to the possible dangers. Brushing her fears aside, she stopped in front of him.

He gaze slowly drifted upwards.

Their eyes locked.

Hers, warm, but apprehensive.

His, cold, gazing towards some distant place called hope.

He slowly moved his foot and jogged the tiny tin. It only had a few coins in it.

'There's not enough in there to even buy you a MacDonald's,' she whispered.

Their eyes just searched each other once more.

By now Cathy's heart was leaping from her chest, 'I would like invite you to spend Christmas Day with me.' A warmth flooded through her body, but caution still lurked in the background.

*Limoncello – Perry A. Simpson*

His cracked lips struggled to move. She could see that the pain made it difficult for him to speak.

'Why?' he grunted.

'Mother Teresa, 1975', she smiled offering him a helping hand. All fear had fled her for the moment, 'I'm not taking no for an answer,' she insisted.

'It's not the best offer I have had you know,' he joked.

○‿○

'First thing's first. You can go and have a bath to freshen up a little. There's a pair of my jeans and a sweatshirt that should fit you,' she pointed him towards the bathroom at the end of the hall.

He just nodded and shuffled slowly on the cedar laminate flooring.

Cathy's mind drifted back to reality again. She realised that she had no idea who he was and now he was in her bathroom. She had let a complete stranger into her house and was now starting to regret this act of foolishness.

Cathy went into the kitchen and hid the knife rack in the food cupboard.

He had been a long time now, she thought.

Had he committed suicide?

Taken an overdose?

Was he laying a blood filled bath?

Was he planning how to rape and kill her?

Panic had started to rage through her mind when the dirty smelly old tramp, that had entered the bathroom nearly an hour ago, reappeared a clean shaven handsome gentleman.

He's a clean killer, she thought.

As he slowly drew closer she noticed the redness in his bloodshot eyes.

Cathy's chin dropped. Her body started to shake as he moved in closer. Her eyes were beginning to flood.

*Limoncello – Perry A. Simpson*

He suddenly threw his arms around her neck, his strong grip lifting her off the ground, swinging her round in a slow pirouette. His body shook violently as he wept unreservedly.

'Richard?' she whispered, kissing him on his cheek.

# The Nun

Harry Stockwell quickly ran to his car and jumped in. The rain hammered down onto the roof of the recently polished Silver Mercedes. Another night with a Pizza and Stella, he thought. This had become his regular Saturday night. In the distance he noticed a solitary dark figure stood at the Wood Green bus stop. Feeling charitable he decided to stop and offer a lift.

Despite creeping slowly to a stop, the motion of the car created a light wave in a puddle that splashed up onto the pavement.

'Can I offer you a lift?'

'Bless you my son.'

Harry's jaw dropped as a Nun climbed into the passenger seat.

'Sister Geraldine,' she said turning to acknowledge his good deed. 'You are?'

'Harry. Just call me Harry.'

Harry couldn't stop staring at her face – it was the most beautiful face he had ever seen. He felt an embarrassing lump growing in his groin.

∽∞∽

Sister Geraldine sat quietly grasping her little black bible.

The rainfall was heavier. The wiper blades struggled to keep the windscreen clear. Despite this, Harry was finding it hard to concentrate. He became increasingly distracted

## The Nun

as a life-long fantasy resurrected itself. He glanced down at her long legs hidden away from temptation by a black robe, held tightly together, in the middle by a white rope. Sex with a women dressed as a Nun was top of his list, but she is actually a Nun.

'Where to Sister?'

'Anywhere along the High Street will be fine, thank you.'

Harry Stockwell had just turned thirty nine and was still single. He had never been very good when it came to engaging with the fairer sex. The occasional one-night stand after heavy night down the Fox and Duck or an overindulgent encounter with an expensive prostitute was the norm.

Harry couldn't stand the stoney silence any longer. 'It appears the heavens have opened up tonight Sister.'

Sister Geraldine glared at him.

'Oops! Sorry Sister. I didn't mean to be disrespectful.'

'Well, you could have said that it is pissing down,' she replied with a smile.

The stoney silence returned. Harry couldn't imagine why someone so beautiful would want to become a Nun. Her hazel eyes mounted on her perfect complexion, framed by the modest veil.

What a waste, he thought. His eyes began to wonder to gaze downwards once more. He relived his old fantasy, imagining running his hand up the length of her thigh. He visualised the moment when he would discover what lingerie would greet him when the robe fell to the floor. In his previous encounters he assumed that it must be all black, but this was a mature version and the reality might be that the nun concealed a naughty little secret beneath the robe. This, a rebellious act against the dignity and simplicity to the nature of her vocation.

Sister Geraldine turned to Harry, 'What are you doing tonight?'

*Limoncello – Perry A. Simpson*

Harry was abruptly brought back to reality. He wasn't quite sure how he should answer. He could hardly say he was going for the 3 P's – pint, pizza and a prostitute.

'A quiet night in with a pizza, a few beers and a good movie.'

'Which movie may I ask?'

'Two mules for Sister Sara.'

'Is it a religious movie?'

Harry felt himself blushing. Of all the bloody movies I could have chosen, he grimaced.

'No, it's a western movie about a Sister with two mules.'

Sister Geraldine smirked crossing her leg over, forcing her robe to ride upwards and revealing her pale leg.

Harry momentarily lost control of the car, clipped the kerb narrowly avoiding a green wheelie bin, before correcting his position on the road.

The temptation was too great and Harry very cautiously placed his hand on her thigh.

Sister Geraldine didn't even flinch.

Harry slowly slid his hand up her thigh.

'Now Harry, remember Luke 14:10.'

'I am so sorry Sister. I do not know what came over me.'

'Watch and pray so that you will not fall into temptation. The spirit is willing, but the flesh is weak,' Sister Geraldine quoted, showing Harry the Bible.'

Harry should have felt completely ashamed of himself, but instead, he wanted to give in to temptation again.

Sister Geraldine shifted in her seat causing the robe to ride a little higher up her thigh.

Harry's hand hovered over her thigh once more. He just had to do it. It would be a story to tell the lads tonight. He would earn much respect for this truly devilish act. His hand came into contact with her smooth, silky skin. He felt a warm glow embrace him and to his surprise his hand had made it up her thigh to her slip.

*Limoncello – Perry A. Simpson*

'Now Harry, I must protest. Remember Luke 14:10.'

'Sister, please forgive me. I don't what has come over me tonight.'

'Could be the weather?' Sister Geraldine laughed.

Harry had no idea what Luke 14:10 said, but he felt satisfied that he hadn't let this opportunity pass him by. Although, he had only partly fulfilled his fantasy, he was remorseful, but not too much.

⁂

The rain had stopped, the sun had reappeared to unveil a glorious mid-summer's evening. The road was already beginning to dry in places.

'You can drop me here Harry if would.'

She very elegantly slide across the seat and climbed out of the car. 'Thank you for the lift.'

'Your more than welcome Sister and my apologies again for my disgraceful behaviour.'

'Think nothing of it. Maybe we could do this again sometime.' She handed Harry her bible. 'Luke 14:10 Harry.' She laughed and gently closed the door.

Harry looked at the little modern looking bible somewhat confused. There was a marker in a page. He opened it. It flew out of the page at him – Luke 14:10

> "But when you are invited, go and sit down in the lowest place, so that when he who invited you comes he may say to you, 'Friend, go up higher.' Then you will have glory in the presence of those who sit at the table with you."

He glanced across the street to see the Nun stood in a queue with a Devil. Above the door of the building, "Fancy Dress Party" screamed at him in bold white lettering.

*Limoncello – Perry A. Simpson*

Sister Geraldine smiled, accompanied with a cheeky little wave.

*Limoncello – Perry A. Simpson*

## *Pepper*

Thomas Henry placed his rucksack in the overhead locker and took his seat adjacent to a very elegant, elderly woman.

Their eyes met briefly.

She had long well groomed brown hair, charming blue eyes, and pale clear skin tone.

He guessed that she was in her early sixties and probably wealthy judging by the quality of the jewellery on display.

Thomas made himself comfortable with a book he had bought for the flight. He was not sure whether he would be able to read it. His mind was elsewhere.

Before he had taken this work assignment in Shanghai, his relationship with Amelia was following the expected route of setting up home and starting a family with all the usual commitments of mortgage, marriage, and mayhem of the little patter of tiny feet. This chartered path of life was about to become derailed.

He had fallen for a beautiful Asian angel.

⁓∞⁓

'You look troubled.'

Thomas glanced up to find the elegant passenger staring at him through the divider that separated their private booths.

'Yes. Not really looking forward to going home.'

'I know that feeling,' she smiled. 'My name is Tina by the way,' offering her hand across the screen.

'Thomas, but everybody calls me Tom.'

'Nice to meet you Tom.'

Tom acknowledged her with a smile.

'So Tom, are you going to let me know what that glum face is all about.'

Tom didn't know this women at all, yet, he felt at ease with her. She was a bit like his dearly departed grandma. He could talk to her about anything.

'OK, I'll start,' she smiled. 'Let me guess. You're not wearing a wedding ring so it must be girlfriend trouble? You're in a long-term relationship back home and you have met someone here in China? How am I doing so far?'

God, she's just like Grandma, he thought.

'Yes, is it that obvious?'

'My dear, when you get to my age, being married for nearly fifty years, you have raised kids and seen them grow up and make all the mistakes you did, then yes, it is obvious.'

Tom was taken aback. 'I don't want you to take this the wrong way, but you remind of my grandma. She seemed to know everything.'

'None taken Tom.'

'You are right. I have been seeing this girl, Marian, for about five years now. She is wonderful, but it's like we are already married. The fun seems to gone out of our relationship.'

'You mean the sex is crap?'

'Well, if put like that, then, Yes.'

'Tom my dear boy. There something you need to understand about women; they are complicated. You spend a lifetime trying to understand them and never succeed. Men are easily pleased, women on the other hand, are always striving for more.'

Tom frowned.

*Limoncello – Perry A. Simpson*

'Take my Jack. We met on the Piccadilly line, had great sex, fell love, got married and the sex was reduced to a weekly Sunday night quickie. Then, sadly, he died.' A tiny tear escaped from her left eye.

Tom placed his hand on hers.

She smiled and quickly brushed away the tear.

'So what brought you to China?'

A smile erupted across her face, 'Leonardo.' At which point she sneezed violently making Tom jump.

Tom smiled.

'When Jack died I was lost. It was at that point I realised it just how much I loved him and I would never find anyone that could replace him.' Another tear worked itself free.

Tom squeezed her hand gently. 'Leonardo?'

'Yes, the Spanish Flamenco Maestro, and stallion in the bedroom!' Tina released several violent sneezes followed by a very deep groan and ending with a gentle sigh.

Tom released her hand.

'We met at a hotel in Beijing. There was a Flamenco class for beginners and I thought why not give it a go. That's where I met him. He guided me round the dance floor. He could make a women with one leg look good.'

There was a pause as Tina's mind drifted and Tom worked out how to ask the obvious.

'Yes Tom, we had sex, every night, almost all night. For nearly fifty years I had thought that I had an orgasm and then Leonardo came along and hit the G spot.'

Tom started to blush.

'We explored everything, did things I would never have dreamed of with Jack.' Tina released several more violent sneezes followed by a very deep groan and ending with a really deep passionate sigh.

'Are you alright?'

'I am Fine – Thank you Tom.'

She took a sip of water. Her eyes were soft and glazed.

*Limoncello – Perry A. Simpson*

'Tom, life is too short. You are still young and have plenty to look forward to. You are a very attractive young man and I can't imagine you being alone for very long,' She said winking at him.

Tom was beginning to feel uncomfortable.

'Relax Tom, I am not making a play for you. It sounds like you already have your hands full and are going home for a rest.'

Tom grimaced.

'It is now that I realise what I had in Jack. With him I was strictly missionary and he was too much of gentlemen, wouldn't have dreamed of doing what Leonardo does in the bedroom.'

Tina released several more violent sneezes followed by a another deep groan, ending with another deep and passionate sigh.

'Seriously, are you alright?' Tom asked.

'I have a rare condition called "Sneeze-gasm".'

'Is it serious?'

'No, but can be embarrassing at times. Especially, if I have a full orgasm after I sneeze. You know, down there?'

Tom frowned and looked away.

'Nice though. It is a shame that I cannot control it.'

'Are you taking any medication for it?'

'Yes, black pepper.'

Tom looked at her is disbelief, 'Pepper, how does that help?'

Tina let out a raucous laugh, shaking violent, rolling back and forth.

She tapped Tom gently, 'You should see your face. Sorry Tom, I couldn't resist.'

'You're just winding me up?' he sighed.

'Yes.' She continued to laugh.

Tom started laughing too, 'Sneeze – what was it?'

*Limoncello – Perry A. Simpson*

'Sneeze-gasm. It just an urban legend that if you sneeze seven times in a row you will orgasm.'

'So why the sneezing fits?'

'Bloody air conditioning makes me sneeze. I faked the orgasm bit.'

'Leonardo?'

'No, not really a replacement for my Jack. I just fly to Beijing twice a year for break and get Leonardo to dance and fuck my brains out.'

Tom chuckled.

'Cheaper than an escort Tom.'

Tom shook his head.

'There's a moral in all this Tom, let me know when you find it.'

## Drunk

Time please ladies and gentlemen.' The chunky barman, Mike Taylor, rang the bell three times.

'What happened to last orders?' a voice shouted from the crowd.

'You drank it.'

The room erupted into laughter.

Mike pointed to a solitary figure bridging the gap between his bar stool and the bar top.

'Who is he?' Steve replied.

'No idea. He staggered in here around six o'clock.'

'How many has he had?'

'Too many.'

The crowd slowly dispersed, the empties collecting on the bar.

'Time to go sir.'

The lonely figure raised his glass, and requested another.

'Sorry, it is time for you to leave now, sir.'

He responded with a polite two-fingered salute and while attempting to dismount the stool, fell flat on his face.

'Would you like me to call a taxi sir?'

'No. I only live round the corner – I can manage thank you.'

The drunk man then lunged from table to table until he reached the door.

## Drunk

Once outside the drunk wrestled into his brown crumpled jacket and shuffled along a low wall until he reached the corner where he lost his balance and fell over the wall and into the adjacent garden. Now that he had fallen in the garden, he decided to take a short cut and crawled slowly, across the lawn, through the flower bed to the opposite wall. Exhausted by this tactical manoeuvre, the drunk paused before hauling himself to his feet and steadied himself on the wall.

The temperature had dropped and a light rain dusted the pavements.

Having caught his breath, he staggered on along the low wall, muttering to himself. When the wall ended, he paused and studied the way ahead. He shuffled his feet before making a mad dash to the lamp post, tripped, and fell forward just enough to cling onto the lamp post.

'What the …?'

He used the lamp post to slowly haul himself back onto his feet.

'Thank you kind sir,' he said to the lamp post. He re-aligned his body and embarked on another leap of faith, heading straight for the next lamp post some 25 metres on.

---

Parked up across the street two police officers watched the gala performance of the drunk with his repertoire from the Ministry of silly walks.

'Take a look at this idiot – Can you believe this?' PC Jones said, leaning forward.

'He is completely hammered. Look his legs have turned to jelly,' laughed PC Holland.

They watched in amazement as the drunk performed the cross between a limbo and break dance, spinning around a rubbish bin and plunging into a large privet hedge, only to to get thrown back again.

*Limoncello – Perry A. Simpson*

'Why do they do it?', PC Jones exclaimed.

'Beats me,' Holland replied.

With knees touching, the drunk waddled like a penguin with perfection, his body completely synchronised with his bandy legs. He made great progress until he reached the kerb, misjudged the height difference and dropped like a sack to the wet tarmac.

'Oops, there he goes,' Jones laughed. Both officers laughed uncontrollably.

Unable to lift himself without the aid of something upright, the drunk crawled across the slippery surface where he was greeted by a blue disabled parking sign. This, he used to guide himself back to an upright position. Without further ado, he spiralled the post. Holding his arm out for balance he appeared to skip around the pole.

'Look, he thinks he's Gene Kelly now,' Holland laughed. 'Maybe, he should audition for Britain's Got Talent.'

PC Jones started to sob with laughter.

The drunk was now but a few feet from their parked car. They watched as he did a quick step to the adjacent tree, where he paused and searched for the zip of his trousers. Having found it, he seem to do a Michael Jackson Billie Jeans legs impression as he struggled with the zip. He stood motionless and he watered the base of the tree unaware that he had a audience, PC Jones and PC Holland.

'Come on, the show's over.'

PC Holland opened the door and got out. PC Jones reluctantly followed.

'Good evening sir,' PC Holland said confronting the drunk.

'Arr, they you are,' the drunk replied.

'What's your name?'

'Can't remember. Had one when I came out. Lost it now.' He swayed back and forth.

'Can you show me some ID sir?' PC Jones asked.

*Limoncello – Perry A. Simpson*

After slapping his right hip four times, he produced his wallet from his trouser pocket. 'Wasn't me officer honest.'

PC Jones opened the wallet, 'No driving license.' He flicked through his credit cards and took out a single card. 'Can you confirm that you are Mr. J. White.'

'Yes officer, I confess it is my wallet.'

The two officers exchanged a disapproving glance.

'Where do you live Mr. White.'

'Please call me Ducky. Oh no, that's not it. Jimmy. Yes, that's it. Jimmy.'

'Right Jimmy where do you live?'

'Not here.'

'Yes, we know that.'

White lost his balance and fell back against the tree, 'Lucky you were there my friend,' he said addressing the tree. 'My legs aren't what they used to be you know.'

PC Jones's patience was wearing thin.

'Look, we need to confirm where you live.'

'In a house with big old blue door.'

'Yes, the address?'

'I don't need your address. I don't even know you.'

'No, Jimmy we need your address.'

'Ah mine, sorry. Yes, of course. Denton Manor'

PC Jones sighed. 'We had better bundle him in the back and get him home.'

'I agree, we'll be all night processing the paperwork.'

PC Holland opened the nearside passenger door and they helped him into the back seat.

---

'Denton Manor is not far, but there is no way he would have made his way back there in this state.'

PC Holland nodded in agreement.

From what they could see Jimmy was an ordinary middle-aged guy, dressed well and obvious not short of money. He wasn't one of the regular unruly drunks they often encountered at this time of night. So, he got a free ride home and not a night in a cell.

PC Holland pulled into the drive and followed it's half mile lead to a sweeping cobbled courtyard.

PC Holland jumped out and opened the nearside passenger door. Jimmy fell out of the opposite door.

Both PCs helped him to his feet and guided him to the big old blue door.

Jimmy amazingly produced a set of keys and handed them to PC Jones.

Once inside, PC Jones turned on the lights.

Jimmy farted.

'Let's put him in here,' PC Holland exclaimed.

They dragged him over the lounge and gently lowered him down onto the soft brush suede sofa.

'Thank you kind sirs.'

Upon hearing the commotion, an elderly lady appeared at the door.

'What the blooding hell ... Sorry officers.'

'Mrs White, we found him roaming around in the streets.'

She looked a bit confused. 'Have you been drinking again Jimmy.'

'Of course, my little twig. Only two bottles.'

'Wine?' PC Jones asked.

'No – Whiskey.'

The two PC's looked sternly at Mrs White.

'Thank you for bringing him back safely. Hope he wasn't too much trouble.'

'Not a problem Mrs White.'

'Where did you leave his wheelchair,' she inquired.

PC Jones looked over at is colleague, then back at Mrs White, 'What wheelchair?'

*Limoncello – Perry A. Simpson*

# Hair Raising

Sofia was looking forward to her holiday in Greece. It had been a long week and now it was Saturday, which meant she would be finished by twelve thirty. It was bright outside, but the sudden rush of cold air through the door was a subtle hint that autumn was on its way. The buzzer squealed erratically as the door opened and then closed again.

'At last, a customer,' Sofia announced.

'I was beginning to think we weren't going to get any today,' Tracy replied.

'I believe it's your turn.'

A tall, very well-built man stood at the counter by the door. His dark shoulder length hair was gathered together with a tatty red hair band. He had beautiful electric blue eyes, which lit up his rather weathered complexion. Sofia adored blue eyes and fell in love with them instantly.

---

'Please, take a seat,' Sofia asked softly.

At first he hadn't registered her request. She swiped the seat with the gown to remove any loose hair.

'Oh, sorry,' he responded, quickly leaping into the red leather chair.

His voice was soft, but Sofia detected a hint of nervousness in his tone. She also noticed how he had flinched as she tightened the gown around his neck. His faded denim jeans that appeared to be too tight around the waist and his T-shirt carried a badly faded motif, the sleeves had been roughly cropped just past his shoulders. Sofia observed how his hair was badly matted and riddled with dead ends. Despite this bedraggled appearance, she could almost taste, as well as smell, the clean aroma that surrounded his presence, not scented, just clean.

Sofia ran her hands through his hair. A strange feeling of warmth worked its was down through her body, as though touching him had ignited something inside her. He intrigued her, stirring strange emotions deep inside her body.

'How would you like me to cut it?'

'Just a number two please, front and back, blending it in at the sides.'

'Are you sure?'

'Yes.'

'Really? You want the lot cutting off?'

'New look,' he smiled.

Sofia frowned and reached for the electric trimmer. The dull buzz from the trimmer oscillated as Sofia worked across his scalp. Great lumps of hair tumbled to the floor. She could see the perspiration forming through the back of his t-shirt. He smiled at her in the reflection of the mirror, causing her emotions to boil.

༺༻

She was in the shower with him. His strong arms wrapped around her. Water washed over the eagle tattoo at the top of his arm. She could feel his stiffness developing between her cheeks.

She gently bit his left arm that was keeping her safe.

He slowly rubbed her groin with his strong right hand.

Sofia gasped, the water gently trickling from her mouth.

They adjusted their posture slightly.

*Limoncello – Perry A. Simpson*

She could feel him stiffening between her legs.

They were both breathing more heavily.

He worked his fingers in deeper, feeling the warmth inside her. Sofia was right on the edge. One careless movement of his hand and she would climax, long before he was ready.

He could sense it and slowly withdrew, following the curvature of her body, using it as a guide to her firm breasts, exploring magnetism of her nipples. He gently kissed the top of her head.

She leant back to rest her head on the side of his neck.

~~~

The squeal of the door buzzer and another customer brought her quickly back to reality.

It was another man, much taller, younger and thinner with short black hair. He wore a tatty old red Levis T-short, dirty denim jeans with spotless pure white Nike trainers.

Tracy guided him into next available red chair.

As Sofia glanced up to look at Tracy in the mirror, she noticed how her customer was now watching Tracy's every movement. He was not watching what she doing with the other man's his hair, but was focusing on her.

It made Sofia feel tense. The hairs on the back of her neck began to stand on end and the atmosphere had become colder. Then, she noticed the mean-looking eyes of the younger man glaring at her.

'Is that enough off the sides?' Sofia asked, drawing her customers attention away from Tracy. His bright blue eyes locked onto her and simply nodded.

'What would you like me to do with this?' asked Tracy.

'Show no mercy,' he grunted. His gaze disengaged from Tracy looking at him in the mirror to focus again on Sofia.

Sofia noticed how the two strangers looked at each other as if quietly acknowledging each other.

*Limoncello – Perry A. Simpson*

'Have you been on holiday this year?' Sofia asked softly.

'Yes, you could call it a sort of a holiday,' he grinned.

As Sofia's worked meticulously to balance and layer his hair, her pulse began to race as her emotions bubbled over once more until the sound of the cash register opening brought her attention back at the task in hand.

'Well, I'm about done here,' Sofia announced. 'Would you like any gel?'

The expression on his face said "no".

Sofia offered a mirror so that he could see the back.

He rolled his head round, inspecting Sofia's work, 'It's been a long time since I have felt this free.' A mischievous grin linked each side of his face.

As Sofia brushed away the loose hair from around his neck, she noticed two unusual jagged scars on his left shoulder blade.

He stood up quickly, handed her a crumpled ten pound note, 'Keep the change.' He paused to smile and swiftly left.

Sofia blushed and was about to relive her little day dream when Tracy shouted.

'Look!' Tracy turned the volume up on the television.

The hairs on Sofia's neck charged with a shock as they watched the breaking news footage containing the photo fits of two men.

They were wanted in connection with a nine-year long hunt as they are believed to have been responsible for the death of twelve women – All the victims were blondes, in their mid twenties from Devon and Cornwall.

Each, carefully selected, hair dressers, seduced in their place of work, murdered by asphyxiation, finally laid to rest peacefully on a bed of white rose petals.

Sofia looked at Tracey.

Another sudden chill flashed down her spine. Earlier, she had a day dream, an intimate day dream with a complete stranger. Not any stranger, but a rough looking individual

*Limoncello – Perry A. Simpson*

that sat in her chair while she gave his new look. Sofia remained frozen to the spot, unable to speak, as though paralysed by a predator.

'What do you think?'

'No, they would have mentioned the tattoo,' Sofia lied.

Sofia felt uneasy. She realised that Tracy and her were the only two people who knew what they looked like now – They were also blondes. Both were hairdressers. Her heart pounded as she reached for the phone. The line was dead.

*Limoncello – Perry A. Simpson*

# Nine Lives

Franky "The Metal" Tomasso was sat opposite Mikey "The Dust" Rice. They both bent down low so that they couldn't be heard and to limit the chance of lip reading using CCTV.

'Mikey, you get out of this can next week and you have unfinished business with that little punk banker. Remember, the one you failed to whack ten years ago.'

Mikey nodded slowly.

'Ten years in a place like this can change a man. I hope you haven't become a weak sister or discovered religion.'

Mikey was offended by this remark. He hadn't turned to religion and if anything, he was long overdue for a kill.

Both sat upright.

Franky slid him a book across the table.

Their eyes acknowledged the deal.

Franky pushed the chair back, stood up and walked to the door. At the door he turned, glanced over at Mikey, issuing the coded threat.

⁓∞⁓

Mikey "The Dust" Rice was just a low life villain who had a list of convictions for small time offences, nothing substantial, until he got caught in a job that went bad for Franky "The Metal" Tomasso.

In order, to clear his debt to Franky, he had to perform a little task – Kill a nobody banker living nowhere special. Why? Well, that was a word you never used in the presence of Franky. He had no choice, but to complete what he started ten years ago. The book contained all the details, in code, hidden within the text on specific pages. A simple, but effective cipher that had foiled many who had attempted to crack it. He had about three minutes before it would be confiscated.

---

David Axion, formerly Joe "the Abacus" O'Reilly, stood in front of the tree where ten years ago he had cheated death. He had turned his back and tried to walk way from Frank Tomasso and his is crooked dealings. The price for this was death.

Ten years on, he was surprised that he was still alive to tell the tale and he would often show off the scar on his forehead, where the bullet had deflected before embedding itself deep within in the remains of the tree that stood behind him. He had assumed that Franky had perhaps uncharacteristically let it drop, rather than risk the attempt being linked to his organisation.

The stout, bald-headed figure looked at the lifeless-looking tree. His round-rimmed glasses steamed up as he sipped cold beer from the small green bottle.

A year ago he had attempted the ancient Roman art of pollarding, removing the upper branches of a tree to promote a dense head of foliage and branches. As a banker his money laundering skills were legendary, but this idyllic life style in his rural French retreat wasn't working out quite as he had expected. A local farmer had convinced him that the tree had to go. This meant cutting down the tree and using explosives to remove the stump.

---

*Limoncello – Perry A. Simpson*

'Keep an eye on Mikey. If he fails to complete the job, then you will have to clean up. Either way, take care of Mikey – permanently,' Franky Tomasso demanded. The tall, dark haunched figure, Billy "The Horse" Shoe nodded and left.

⁂

David had dug bore holes around the perimeter and the next task would be to insert the sticks of dynamite down the holes, one-by-one. He returned to his laptop, 'Well, in the youtube video, the tree was slightly larger. So, I guess this should be enough to remove this stump.' David started to insert the sticks of dynamite down each bore hole as shown.

'Not sure how many I need,' he muttered to himself, adding a couple more for luck.

⁂

Laying in undergrowth, Mikey "The Dust" Rice watched his target as he did so ten years ago. 'He will not be so lucky this time,' he grimaced. Seeing the dynamite gave him an idea. He grinned as he adjust the site of his rifle on the first bore hole.

'A tragic accident my friend.'

⁂

Not too far away, the tall haunched figure stood and waited patiently, with Mikey "The Dust" Rice and the David Axion within range. He knew he was best placed to finish the job whatever the scenario. He made one final check for each kill, just to be sure.

⁂

*Limoncello – Perry A. Simpson*

Unaware of the danger he was in, David continued preparing the explosives. Feeling proud of himself, he raised his bottle of 1644 in the air and took a large gulp.

As he walked around the tree, it struck him that he was about to blow away what remained of that almost fateful day. He didn't know why, but he walked back to the very spot where he had been shot. An untimely crack, caught his attention. David saw a familiar figure lurking in the undergrowth. It was "deja vu". He stood motionless, unable to move. At that point he remembered he was a banker, not a gangster. Still clutching a single stick of dynamite complete with detonator gave him a crazy idea.

Mikey took aim, his sights still on the first bore hole. He straightened his forefinger and pulled back on the trigger. Checking the target in the sight, he took a deep breath.

Meanwhile, David estimated the distance and took a step backwards, getting ready to throw the dynamite.

Mikey seeing the danger, quickly squeezed the trigger and fired.

There was a huge explosion, followed by larger explosions. This lifted the tree, including its roots clean from the ground.

The explosion dislodged the bullet, propelling it through the air into the head of Mikey, killing him instantly.

The series of blasts, as opposed to the single one that David had planned, catapulted the entire tree across the clearing and into the path of the tall haunched figure poised in the bushes.

When the dust and debris had settled. Mikey 'The Dust" Rice was slumped over his rifle, dead. The legs and arms is all that remained of Billy "The Horse" Shoe lay beneath the tree, dead.

*Limoncello – Perry A. Simpson*

David Axion, formerly Joe "the Abacus" O'Reilly, was nowhere to be found.

*Limoncello – Perry A. Simpson*

# *Stomach Pains*

'How long has he had these pains then?' Doris Long asked, shifting her posture on the pale green synthetic leather arm chair.

Gwen looked up. Her teared-stained eyes looked tired. She was tired – tired of living.

'Two years. About two years.'

'Two years?'

She knew that Bob Jackson, Gwen's husband' had been suffering from chronic stomach pains, but hadn't realised just how long it had been until now.

'Yes. Two of the worst years of my life. We have been in and out of this place so many times now. We actually got an invite to Dr. Drummond's leaving do.'

'What the hell have all of the doctors being doing in all that time?'

'Search me Doris. I even think they considered treating him for being boring. Now finally, they have decided to open him up and take a look inside.'

Two tiny tears edged their way out of the corner of each eye.

༄

Doris shifted in the chair. 'Why is it in these places, the chairs only look comfortable. This chair is making the crease between my arse cheeks sweat.'

Gwen wiped her eyes. She looked worried and that was because she was worried. She brushed her greasy auburn hair behind eyes to stop it irritating her tearful blue eyes.

'I know what you mean Doris. Right now, I just want to sleep and wake up to find that this was just a bad dream.'

Doris was a good ten years older, her hair dyed giving off a purple hue. It looked like a giant candy-floss, but firmer. She was known for her directness. If you wanted an honest opinion, then you didn't ask Doris. She would give you a lecture.

'Do you want me to have a word with the doctor?'

'No, Doris it's fine. I am sure Dr. Chong knows what he is doing. He is one of those travelling consultant doctors. He is an expert on abdominal pains.'

'Yes, a Gastro entry something or other ... you know one of those long words that makes you stutter when you try assemble the syllables coherently without sounding like a prat.'

'A gastroenterologist.'

'Exactly. Gastro bla bla ist. Fancy name for someone who looks at yer stomach.'

'He is a physician who specialises in diseases of the digestive system, also called the gastrointestinal (GI) tract. Gastroenterologists have extensive training in the diagnosis and treatment of conditions that affect the oesophagus, stomach, small intestine, large intestine (colon), and biliary system (e.g., liver, pancreas, gallbladder, bile ducts).'

'Is he the one that carries his chop sticks in his top pocket?'

'No, that's Dr. Lou Ling. I don't think they're chop sticks Doris.'

Doris frowned. 'In my day, you went to the doctor where he would give a load pills and some syrup. You only went to the hospital when cutting was involved.'

*Limoncello – Perry A. Simpson*

Gwen smiled. Doris was tiresome with her sarcastic comments and funny little ways, but she also managed to throw in an alternative perspective.

~~~

It had been nearly two hours. Doris had almost finished knitting a new jumper. Gwen had managed to snooze, but was woken by the sound of a pneumatic drill outside.

'Back with us then?' Doris said glaring over the top of their winged-Dame Edna Everage style glasses.

'Yes,' she yawned.

'This Dr. Chong, what will he be looking for?' asked Doris.

'No idea. Something. Anything. The reason for acute abdominal pains.'

'Must be something he's eaten.'

'Yes Doris, I am sure the doctors have considered that. It's nausea, weakness, diarrhoea that go with the abdominal pains that seems to be keeping them guessing.'

'Your Bob hasn't half lost some weight'

'He is a bit skinny now.'

'Well, I've seen more fat on a cold chip.'

'It's due to the constant fatigue and loss of appetite'

'Oh Yes, your Bob was such a active guy, Rugby wasn't it?'

'Yes Doris, he used to play for the local Rugby team. Now, he only plays it on the X-Box. Even that seems to tire him out.'

Doris leapt to her feet, 'Hey Doctor! Come here please.'

'No Doris leave it please.'

The doctor came over. 'Yes, how can I help you?'

'Turn round.'

'What?'

'Just turn round,' Doris insisted.

*Limoncello – Perry A. Simpson*

Not knowing why the Doctor turned round.

Doris offered the knitted jumper to his back.

'What do you reckon Gwen? He is about the same size as your Bob?'

Gwen lowered a reddening face. She couldn't answer.

'By the time you lot find the cause of little bit of stomach pain, it will fit.'

The comment attracted some attention from other patients and some smiles from the nurses.

Gwen was embarrassed, but she had to admit Doris was actually right and did have a point.

⸺

The surgery had dragged on a lot longer than anticipated. Doris hadn't been joking about the jumper. She now had two sleeves, the front and the back.

'Mrs. Gwen Jackson?'

Gwen's heart began to race, 'Yes.'

'My name is Dr. Chong.' The small Chinese doctor greeted Gwen with a polite bow.

'Is my husband OK?'

'He is in the recovery room. It was a long surgery and he will need lots of rest.'

'Did you find anything?'

'Yes we did,' he smiled very enthusiastically.

His reaction was making Gwen slightly nervous.

'Get on with it man,' Doris interrupted. 'She's been waiting two years for this moment.'

'Quite, I apologise that it has taken this length of time to identify the cause of all your husband's symptoms.'

'And?' Doris added.

'Today, during surgery we removed a 6-metre tapeworm.'

Gwen face dropped.

'It is the biggest I have ever encountered. It did not get picked up, because as in rare cases, the tape worm wasn't

*Limoncello – Perry A. Simpson*

responsible for all of the symptoms. This explains the reason for the erratic nature of the symptoms.'

'Where did he pick up a tapeworm?'

'Most likely cause is through eating raw meat containing tapeworm larvae.'

Gwen sat back down, 'He's going to be alright now.'

'Yes. He will need to take some medication and this will help get his appetite back in a few days.'

'No more Steak Tartare for him,' Doris announced.

'Raw meat? No,' Gwen replied. She looked up at the Doctor, 'He's a stoic vegetarian.'

A hot flush started rise up through her core as realised that it was her who was responsible for his condition. Bob did have some raw meat. She gave it to him in a bean salad. It had been her revenge. He was always going on at her about eating meat, the impact cattle farming was having on the environment and so on. When he forgot her birthday, she snapped. So, she made him a special bean salad.

*Limoncello – Perry A. Simpson*

# Hot Tub

'Don't fuss Mum. I'll be fine. Go on. Go! You'll miss your flight.'

Katie hugged her mother, then they slowly uncoiled and blew a kiss to each other as they separated. Katie wasn't very happy about this house-sitting responsibility. Her father had suddenly become obsessed with home security and had spent a small fortune on motion CCTV, toughened double-glazing, high security locks, and wall spikes around the top of the perimeter wall. However, the state-of-the-art alarm system was on the blink again, which meant that Katie had to house watch while her parents went away for a long weekend.

Katie didn't want to spend time alone in this huge house, so she invited a few friends to stay for the weekend. She had a couple of hours before they arrived to prepare food, chill the beer and the wine. Her parents would be none the wiser – They would be in New York.

༄

Katie Bryce was in her early twenties and already divorced. Her first marriage had been a disaster, leaving her with very low self-esteem and adrift in the world. She was an attractive, intelligent woman and didn't really want for anything. Yet, she felt the need to constantly seek recognition from everyone and justify herself. She'd even held on to her married name.

∽∞∽

The door bell rang.

'Hi Katie, you're looking very good.' Gary Meadows gave her huge hug and handed over some flowers.

'This is Dawn. You did say bring a friend?'

'Yes.'

Anyone but Dawn Gibbons. Good start, she thought.

The door bell rang again and Katie was pleased to see one of her former boyfriends, Peter Brooks, who had brought Linda Stark with him. All she needed now was her latest man, David Trundle, to turn up and the partying could begin. He was late as usual.

∽∞∽

The sun beat down on them as they rested in the hot tub. They had consumed the feast that Katie had prepared and moved onto a cocktail of alcohol.

'Lovely place your parents have here.'

'Yes, it's not bad for a man who started off selling Tupperware in a market.'

'Look, I've gone all wrinkly,' exclaimed Dawn.

'You'll were always a bloody prune,' Katie muttered under her breath.

'A bit security conscious your parents?' Peter asked.

'Well, only the best for my father.'

'We'll be very safe in here,' Linda added.

'A bit like a prison. Can't get in or out,' Gary smirked. 'Anyone for more drinks?'

Gary leapt up and headed for the kitchen.

Everyone remained silent soaking up the sun peaking from behind the clouds.

'Hey, Look what I found.'

'Not my father's Lanson Magnum Black Label.'

'Time to really party.'

*Limoncello – Perry A. Simpson*

'Careful with that door Gary. The catch is a little dodgy.'

Too late the latch on the patio door dropped, leaving them locked out, with no way back in.

The temperature dropped as the sky darkened. Large spots of rain pebble dashed the patio.

Everyone wanted to run for cover.

ぐ∞っ

Katie looked at Peter, 'We're stranded in our swim gear and our clothes are inside, what do we do now?'

'Spare key?'

'Back at my flat. It's a Bank holiday and both the neighbours are away for the weekend.'

'What about calling your parents?'

'My phone is inside and anyway, they are on a flight to New York.' Katie snapped.

Everyone sat in silence in the tub while the rain gained momentum.

Gary jumped out, 'We'll have to break in.'

He picked a huge rock and threw at the patio door. It bounced back smashing a large ornate plant pot.

'Now look what you've done,' Katie shouted. 'You won't break the glass.'

'Well, we can't just sit her all night,' Dawn screamed.

'Shut up Dawn.'

Gary walked to the wall and threw a towel over the spikes.

'I'll go to the house opposite to get help.'

Peter helped Gary build a makeshift ladder using garden furniture. Gary started to scale the 2 metre wall and almost reached the top. He slipped, caught himself on a spike and tumbled down the other side of the wall, leaving his shorts still attached to one of the spikes.

*Limoncello – Perry A. Simpson*

## Hot Tub

⚘

Unperturbed, Gary staggered across the road, heading for the house opposite, blood pouring from several bad cuts. The rain washed the blood down his body.

He stood, naked, in a trail of blood ringing the door bell constantly.

No answer.

He saw the curtains move. He began pounding on the glass door with his fist.

⚘

It had been a good twenty minutes and no sign of help. Sirens in the distance began to draw closer. Katie had a bad feeling about this. They all remained planted in the hot tub. Blue flashing lights reflected all around the neighbouring buildings. A fireman's ladder appeared over the top of the wall. One-by-one the fireman hauled them to the other side of the wall.

They were greeted by armed Police officers who directed them to sit of the ground with the hands on their heads. A dog handler walked past sniffing for drugs.

Katie saw Gary sitting on the floor in cuffs, his wounds being tended to by a paramedic.

⚘

It took an hour for the Police to establish that Gary wasn't some crazed murderer and contacted a local locksmith to come and open the door.

The scene had cleared and only Katie remained with PC Locke and Eddie, the locksmith wearing a black T-shirt with "Keep Calm – I am a Locksmith"

He chuckled continually to himself as he drilled out the barrel.

*Limoncello – Perry A. Simpson*

'PC Locke, will my parents get into trouble over this?'

Eddie burst out laughing uncontrollably. Tears rolled down his cheeks, the laugher turned to a feeble sobbing, followed by the temporarily loss of ability to grip the screw driver with his hands.

'We are not intending to press any charges.'

'Oh good. That's all they'll need when the get back from New York.'

Katie's mobile rang.

'Hi Mum. Having nice time?'

PC Locke looked at Katie.

'Yes, but we did have a bit of panic.'

Eddie started to chuckle again.

'Well, I had to get a locksmith to change the lock on the front door.'

PC Locke started to pace up and down.

'Mum, I do not have a spare key – remember?'

Katie's face suddenly dropped. She walked over to the large clay plant pot. She reached under the foliage of a miniature tree and located a key – the spare key her parents had left in case of an emergency.

'Bit late now' Eddie handed her the new set of keys.

PC Locke sighed.

Eddie started to chuckle again as gathered his tools and left.

*Limoncello – Perry A. Simpson*

# *Blood Night*

Emily Rae had invited her best friends, Beryl, Ethel and Janet, to a cottage in a remote location in the Fens. They decided to have a horror movie night, something they had been doing since they first met as young teenage girls. Retirement had brought the old gang closer together, usually over a pot of tea or two at the Cobbler's Tea Room in Main Street. Emily Rae was the most adventurous and seemed to be always surrounded by chaos and drama. She seemed to be addicted to it and this obsession with adventure has landed her in trouble on more than one occasion. Tonight she had dragged her friends out of their cosy homes, to a remote cottage in the middle of the Fens, miles from anywhere. Innocent enough.

❦

A solitary figure was slumped awkwardly on the grass verge, blood seeping into the undergrowth.

The heavy clouds descended upon the flat, damp, low-lying agricultural region.

❦

'So what are we watching then Emily?' Beryl asked, taking charge.

'It's called Blood Night: The Legend of Mary Hatchet.'

'What's it about?' Ethel asked.

'An axe murderer.' Janet responded.

'How do you know? Have you already seen it?' Beryl sighed.

'Only the trailer – looks promising.'

Emily Rae loaded the DVD player, then turned out all the lights for maximum effect.

All four ladies quickly became glued to the large Ultra HD flat screen TV. They were in complete darkness, only the flickering light from the television produced spontaneous bursts of light and shadows around the room.

'What was that?' Beryl asked.

'Sorry ladies, that was me. I've had wind all day,' Emily replied.

'Sure you haven't shit yourself?'

The ladies shuffled around to try and avoid the unpleasant aroma.

Once settled, they were all glued to the plot as a group of teenagers prepared for their Blood Night party with a séance at Mary's grave at a cemetery on Sweet Hollow Road in Huntington. One of the teenager's told one of the stories related to her by the cemetery caretaker. He was a former King's Park employee who claimed that Mary would keep coming back to kill until she found her child, who was buried in a shallow grave near Kings Park.

They watched intently as the teenagers proceeded to a party at a house, where guests had been strangled by an unseen murderer amidst supernatural occurrences.

'Bit slow isn't?' Ethel exclaimed.

'Shush.'

'Why is it always so dark? You can't see anything,' she continued.

'Ethel will you shush. It's meant to be dark. It adds to the effect – makes it more realistic,' Janet snapped.

Ethel pulled a face.

She received three more disapproving looks.

The four ladies remained quite still, not daring to move.

*Limoncello – Perry A. Simpson*

Each, waiting for that moment when something suddenly happens that would make them all jump out of their skins.

A large flash of lightening cut across the screen.

All four gasped.

―――

Outside, a distant rumble rolled across the sky followed by a violent crack that shook the surrounding area of the cottage. This did not distract the four ladies who remained fixed on the evolving plot.

The teenagers were well into the party, the river of alcohol in full flow, when the lights suddenly went out.

Only the fumbling of the panic stricken teenagers could be heard.

Suddenly, there was a crash outside the cottage.

'Did you hear that?' Beryl gasped.

'Yes, it came from the back.' Emily got up and walked towards the window. She peeled back the edge of the curtain far enough to look out. A flash of lightening lit up the surroundings.

'There's someone coming up the drive,' Emily announced.

'Are you sure?' Beryl challenged.

There was a another fierce flash.

'Oh yes, and he has an axe.'

'Emily, that's not funny,' Ethel protested.

'He's stopped now. Just staring at the house. Blood dripping from his axe.'

'That's enough Emily,' Janet snapped.

Another fierce flash of lightning tore across the dark shadowy sky.

The power went off, plunging the house into complete darkness.

'Everyone remain still. Not a word,' Emily insisted.

The man outside had gone and was no longer visible.

*Limoncello – Perry A. Simpson*

'Can you see him?' Beryl whispered.

'No.'

'What do we do now?' Ethel sniffled.

'Stay very, very still.'

They heard a scraping noise followed the crash of a dustbin lid as the man appeared to stumble.

Emily carefully made her way towards the kitchen.

'What are you doing?' Beryl whispered.

Emily put her forefinger to her lips and waved her hand signalling for them to get down low.

The back door into the kitchen rattled.

Locked.

Emily moved in closer and stood in the darkest spot.

There was a crash as an axe made easy work of removing the glass panel.

A blood-stained hand reached in, felt for the key and slowly unlocked the door. The door squealed as it opened.

Emily held her breath and moved slowly into position.

The glass crunched under the boots as the man entered the kitchen.

Emily made her move. There was an almighty crash followed by a series of screams as she wrestled the intruder onto the kitchen floor.

⁂

Beryl, Ethel and Janet remained glued to their hiding place.

The television bleeped.

'The power's back on,' Beryl whispered.

'Well, don't just stand there. Call the Police!' Emily screamed.

Beryl leapt to her feet and turned the lights on. Ethel and Janet crept towards the the kitchen. They turned the light on.

They saw Emily had the axe man pinned to the ground in some form of armlock.

*Limoncello – Perry A. Simpson*

'I see the Kung Fu classes came in handy then,' Janet laughed.

A sea of sirens and blue flashing lights emerged from the mile long drive to the cottage.

Armed officers stormed the cottage, forcing the ladies to surrender by laying on the ground, hands on their heads.

'Good job I took up yoga,' Ethel grimaced.

'You can release the suspect now,' the officer said, pointing a semi-automatic gun.

Emily released her tight grip on the man.

He groaned as he rolled over onto his back.

'Is this some sort of joke?' The officer glared at Emily. 'This is no axe murderer. This is Tim Bennett the fireman from the local fire station.'

'Well, what was he doing creeping up the drive and smashing his way into the house, then officer?' Emily snapped.

'You stupid women, I was involved in a road traffic accident just up the road,' Tim grunted. 'I came here to raise the alarm.'

'What with a bloody great axe?'

'I borrowed the axe from the station to cut some logs at home. I was on my back to the station to return it.' He gasped. 'This cottage is never occupied at this time of the year. I knew I would need to break in.'

Still surrounded by armed police, Emily got up off the floor with her hands raised.

Beryl, Ethel and Janet stood in silence as they watched Emily being escorted to a Police car – handcuffed.

*Limoncello – Perry A. Simpson*

## *Shredded*

Jane Meadows was really proud when she landed a position at the Turner, Archer, Guardian Royal partnership. Although only temporary at first, it was to be the start of her career and the the route to a PA position in a high profile organisation. Naturally she felt a little anxious. This was a big step. She had been applying for jobs for more than a year without success. She began to wonder if being blonde had anything to with it.

She paused in front of the revolving doors, looked up at the top of the glass building and wondered which floor she would be working on.

She closed her umbrella, entered the foyer and made her way to the reception desk.

༺༻

'This is your desk Jane,'

Patricia showed her to a pokey little cubical, containing the standard medium sized desk with light tan wood effect desktop, matching 3-draw cabinet and free-standing, but matching, filing cabinet.

'Thank you.'

'Your welcome. I suggest you get settled in first and then I will take you for the induction and tour.'

Jane nodded.

'Jane Meadows I assume?'

Jane looked up at the stern looking woman dressed in a

slick silvery jacket and matching trousers that framed her body profile perfectly.

'Yes.' Jane offered her hand.

'My name is Cathy Carter and this …' she paused, pointing across the office, '… is my team.'

Jane glanced across the complex maze of desks, haphazardly separated by low-level, soft royal, blue partitions. She was conscious that all eyes were on her. Cathy Carter's proceeded to do the full body scan.

'Welcome to Turner, Archer, Guardian Royal partnership.'

'Thank you.'

'Jane, the essence of good office etiquette is to be respectful and courteous at all times and with everybody.' She looked Jane straight in the eyes. 'That applies to everyone, except me.'

She lifted her head slightly, turned and waltzed off.

Jane turned to Patricia.

'She's the acting Personal Assistant to Mr Jenkins.'

'What happened to Miss Martin?'

'Promoted.'

'Really?'

'Yes. Miss Cathy Carter thinks she is going to be announced as her replacement.'

'Will she get it?'

'I hope not. She's bright, intelligent and very ambitious. Every office has a bitch. At TAG Royal it is Cathy Carter,' Patricia sighed.

She turned back to face Jane, 'You'll have to watch yourself when dealing with her. Get yourself settled and I'll be back to show you round.'

Jane smiled and placed a Peace Lily in a ceramic pot on her desk. The air was already filled with the sound of rattling keyboards. The rain had eased and there were signs that it might be brightening up outside. Jane took out an

*Limoncello – Perry A. Simpson*

amethyst from her small red bag and placed it next to the PC.

Sitting quietly at her desk, Jane recalled the 'Office Angels' guidance notes on "Body Language" she had received to help her to with the interview. She wondered whether any of the tips would help get her through her first day. It had helped her land this job, but this dream start to her career had hit a snag – Cathy Carter.

༄

Patricia had shown her around the entire building and completed her induction. She had managed to get access to the office network and had already finished preparing some documents for Patricia.

Patricia had returned to Jane's desk, 'All done?'

'Yes.' Jane handed her the three documents.

'Great. thank you.'

'Not bad for a blonde?'

They both laughed.

'What are you two witless wonders doing? Haven't you got anything better to do?'

It was Miss Cathy Carter on her rounds.

'Well, I've been showing Jane around the office and got her started on a few tasks.' Patricia explained.

Jane gave Cathy a prolonged disapproving look. Her bright blue eyes much softer than her manner.

Cathy turned to address Jane, 'I've just taken a peek at your resume. Very impressive. You weren't Miss Martin's choice, but I guess you'll have to do.'

The Office Angels guidance notes stated, "Make sure you reward their efforts with an easy smile." Jane simply smiled, but said nothing in response. She maintained eye contact, so as not to come across as evasive and insecure. Quite the opposite, she fully intended to make Cathy feel insecure.

*Limoncello – Perry A. Simpson*

Unimpressed, Cathy scowled, and took a couple of steps to her left, shifting her gaze back to Patricia.

Jane mirrored Cathy by shuffling to catch her gaze and lull her into a false sense of security by letting her think that there is a connection between them.

'You know what they say about blondes Patricia? She said directing the question away from Jane.

'No, go on enlighten me,' Patricia replied.

'They are woman who rely on looks rather than on their intelligence,' Cathy whispered, throwing a teasing stare in Jane's direction.

'Alfred Hitchcock preferred to cast blonde women for major roles in his films as he believed that the audience would suspect them the least,' Jane countered.

Patricia could not help but raise a smile.

She was not the only one.

This confrontation had caught the attention of the entire office.

'Well little Miss Perfect, I have a nice little job for you. It shouldn't be too difficult, even for an intelligent blonde like you. Sure you can manage it?' Cathy teased.

'Well that would depend on what it is you have in mind for me on my first day,' replied Jane maintaining positive eye contact.

Cathy reached over the screen and handed Jane two unbound reports.

'I want you to make a copy of this report for me. Then, I want you to shred this one. I'll be back in an hour.'

∞

Cathy returned to find Jane standing in front of the shredder. 'Haven't you done that little job yet.'

'Not exactly,'

'Why not?'

*Limoncello – Perry A. Simpson*

'Trying to work out how this damn shredder thingy works'

Cathy stomped angrily across to the print room.

Deathly silence fell upon the office. Everybody appeared to have stopped breathing.

Cathy snatched the report from her, 'It's so simple that even a dumb blonde like you can do it. She slammed the entire document on the feeder of the shredder and hit the "Start".

The machine took the document a one page at time and shredded it at great speed. They watched as the machine ate the last page. 'There you are – Simple.' Cathy looked on victoriously.

'Thanks, but where do the copies come out?'

Cathy's froze as she realised that Jane still had the old copy of the report in her other hand.

*Limoncello – Perry A. Simpson*

# *Sisters*

Patsy O'Keefe had heard about the sudden death of her father and thought that after thirty years there would be little or no pain, but she was suddenly feeling homesick. She was one of two sisters who were once close. She and Cindy were inseparable, like twins, they went everywhere and did everything together.

That was until the blue eyed, curly haired James 'O'Hara came along. From that day their inseparable bond appeared broken and they fought like cats over him. Jealousy and rage replaced the sharing and caring nature of their relationship.

Patsy woke up one morning, boarded a flight to New York and left. She had shut out her past, built a successful business and thought that she would never look back. Now, she was hoping that maybe this tragic loss would allow her and Cindy to become close again and things might return to the way they were.

―∞―

Cindy O'Keefe stood over her father's coffin. It hadn't been easy looking after him all these years and she was grateful that he had died peacefully. She was annoyed that her sister hadn't even made the effort to come to the funeral of her father. Especially as she was the favoured one.

She grimaced, 'Little miss bloody perfect Patsy.'

'Sorry my Lord,' she said quietly under breath.

As she kissed her father on the head, another tear ran down her cheek.

Quite a few people have come to pay their respects, she thought. Her father hadn't been that popular, but they lived in a community where everybody knew everybody and people tended to make your business their business.

In the car she thought about Patsy, remembering the times when they had been thick as thieves. They always knew exactly what the other was thinking, constantly borrowed each other's clothes without asking. If her sister hated someone, she automatically hated them even more. She was the best friend in the world and I couldn't have imagined life without her, she recalled.

When she left home, it was the first time they had been apart and Cindy remembered how she felt almost broken. It was all over a boy, James O'Hara. They both fancied him like mad and that's when the fights started. The split came when she found out that James was seeing Patsy behind her back. Of course, their father took Patsy's side as usual. She had always been his favourite. No matter what. Cindy recalled how she never felt good enough for him and yet, it wasn't good old Patsy that had looked after him all these years. Cindy also remembered how, Patsy leaving they way she did, almost broke his heart. Cindy always knew that, in his eyes, Patsy could do no wrong and that he hoped she would come home one day. She never did. In the end her father had given up all hope and decided to join mum.

Well, now that he has finally past away, Cindy intended to get on with what was left of her life.

She glanced over at her suitcases stacked near the front door.

*Limoncello – Perry A. Simpson*

Patsy was surprised that she hadn't heard anything from her little sister, Cindy. Her father's death had forced her to think about what happened in the past. She hadn't really liked the way her father fussed over her so much. It had been the cause of so much friction between her and Cindy. Surely, now that he was gone, this should just be water under the bridge? As for the boy that had drove her away, She couldn't even remember his name.

'Can I help you? she asked. A tall man, bald had just walked into the reception. He seemed familiar.

'I want to see Natasha,' He insisted.

'Sir, you do know that Natasha is one of our most expensive ladies. Sure you wouldn't prefer someone else?'

'No, I must see Natasha.'

Patsy rang a brass bell and all the girls came into the foyer, scantily dressed in a stunning display of lingerie.

Natasha definitely stood out with pure blond long hair, blue eyes, and her perfectly choreographed figure.

'It will cost you $1,000 for one hour in the penthouse suite.'

The mystery visitor didn't even flinch at the cost and followed the lure of Natasha as she led him up the spiral staircase.

The hour some came and went, yet, the mystery man had not appeared.

Patsy was a little concerned that he might not pay, so sent up some muscle to ensure that everything was in order.

It seemed that he enjoyed his first hour so much that he wanted another $1,000 worth.

This mystery man began to play on Patsy's mind. He did seem familiar, but she could not place him.

Much to her surprise the second hour came and past. As before, she sent up the muscle to collect the payment for the third hour. He paid without fuss or hesitation.

*Limoncello – Perry A. Simpson*

He definitely doesn't seem the type to have that sort of money, thought Patsy.

Natasha had always been a good earner for the house and was paid well hence the very high price tag for her.

───※───

Natasha appeared at the top of the stairs, looking exhausted. The mystery man practically sprinted down the spiral staircase, shirt tails hanging out from his trousers.

'I hope Natasha took good care of you.'

'Oh, yes.' he winked at the tired looking Natasha.

'Natasha is our most expensive girl and no one ever books her for more than one session, but three?'

He smiled, 'Worth $3,000 of anyone's money, don't you think?'

Patsy thought it an odd thing to say. 'Where are you from, may I ask?'

'Ballycastle.'

Patsy looked shocked, 'Ballycastle, Ireland?'

'Yes.'

She suddenly realised why she thought he had seemed familiar, 'James O'Hara?'

'Yes.'

Patsy was in a state of shock. She hadn't seem him in thirty years.

'What the hell are you doing here?'

'Your sister, Cindy, sent me.'

Patsy looked puzzled, 'Why didn't she come herself?'

'Actually, I am acting on behalf of your sister as her solicitor. You are the sole beneficiary in your late father's will. Cindy asked me to send her regards and pass on your $3,000 inheritance in person.'

*Limoncello – Perry A. Simpson*

# Meals on Wheels

Mavis sat quietly tucking into the meal that Dave, her son, had dropped in on his way to work. She was pleased to see that he had sorted himself out after his long-term girlfriend, Maggie, had kicked him out over the parrot saga. How did he know the parrot would blab? Maybe he has finally found something that he can do without getting into trouble, she pondered. Mavis recalled how, as a boy, Dave had always been a bit of dreamer. Lots of fancy ideas to make fast and easy money. His employment career was a catalogue of failures and disasters, She sighed. Longest job he held was that Jason Brown Associates, until he burnt the place down. I do hope this is not just another one of his little hair-brain schemes.

∽∾∽

'This meat's a little tough.' Mavis removed her upper denture and used a cocktail stick to remove some pieces of meat that had lodged onto her gums. She popped the denture back in place and put the half eaten meal on the table.

There was a knock at the door.

'Oh it's you Brenda. Please come on in.'

'How are you Mavis?'

They both went and joined Maggie in Mavis's cluttered lounge.

'Be a love and pop the kettle on would you?'

'Of course.'

Brenda filled the kettle and switched on.

After rinsing the tea pot with hot water, she popped the two tea bags just as the kettle had boiled.

She placed the tray onto the pile of old People's Friend magazines.

'There we are. I didn't realise you were still having your dinner. I would have come later had I known.'

'I'd finished anyway. Meat was too tough for my liking.'

'Where did you get it from – Iceland?'

'No, meals on wheels.'

'I didn't know you got meals of wheels.'

'I don't. Dave drops me in with the occasional meal.'

'How is Dave?'

'You know Dave? Head permanently in the clouds.'

Maggie knew only too well. 'Yes, I am well, well aware of Dave's irritating little habits; football, the horses, women – in that order.'

'Don't be too hard on him Mggie. He means well.'

'It's when he tries to be clever that he gets into trouble.' She remembered how he trained a African Parrot from the local brothel to say some key words, including his own name.

'Well, he has found himself a job doing meals on wheels.'

'Oh good, that'll keep him busy and out of trouble.'

'Well, he seems happy.'

'How are the meals?'

'Not sure about this new menu.'

'Why? What's wrong with it?'

'A bit fancy if you ask me. Too many spices and not enough vegetables. They always over marinate the meat to the point where I can't taste it. What's the point in that I ask you?'

Brenda just nodded – She didn't dare offer her view on the reason for the excessive spice usage.

*Limoncello – Perry A. Simpson*

'Oh great.' Mavis cursed.

'What's wrong?'

'The local gossip is about to pay us a visit. Quick Brenda, go and let her in. Else she'll ring that door bell till the batteries are flat.'

Brenda looked confused.

'She thinks I'm death.'

Brenda smiled and went to open the door.

---

Doreen Cartwright shook her umbrella before entering and placed it on the door mat to dry. She followed Brenda into the lounge.

'Oh, is it raining?' Mavis smiled.

'No, I took a short cut through a car wash.'

Brenda squeezed her a cup of tea from the pot.

'There you are.'

'Thank you. See you didn't eat your meal.'

'No, is that a problem?' Mavis snapped.

'Well, I don't blame you after the story I've just heard.'

Mavis was naturally curious, but she didn't want to encourage the sort of gossip she was into.

'What story?' Brenda inquired.

Mavis made zipping her lips gestures to Brenda.

Maggie stared into the bottom of her empty cup.

Too late.

Doreen accepted the invitation and continued, 'Well, there are rumours doing the usual rounds about the new company doing the meals on wheels menu.'

Brenda threw a look of concern at Mavis.

Mavis grimaced.

'There's been some complaints.'

She paused and placed the palms of her hands on her knees to ensure she had their full attention.

*Limoncello – Perry A. Simpson*

'What sort of complaints?' Brenda asked.

'Surely you don't want to listen to this sort of gossip Brenda?'

Brenda turned to look back at Doreen.

'People are complaining that the food is too spicy.'

'Mavis was just saying the very same,' Brenda interrupted.

Doreen pursed her lips and sat bolt upright, 'Anyways, the new company is under investigation.'

'Don't you mean, they are being questioned about the menu?'

'No, no, no, hygiene.'

Mavis didn't like the sound of this and turned to look out of the window.

'They had to bring in the police.'

Mavis continued staring out the window.

Brenda wasn't sure that she wanted to hear the rest.

'They found a body in one of the freezers.'

That drew Mavis's attention away from the view outside the window, 'What sort of body?'

'A human body.'

'Your kidding?' Brenda gasped.

'Of course she is. Next you'll be telling us that they are serving human flesh in the new meals on wheels menu.'

Brenda glanced over at her unfinished meaty dish.

Doreen looked hurt, but continued, 'They did find a dead cat curled up on a pile of pork chops.'

Brenda, Mavis and Maggie glanced back at Doreen.

'No, they weren't using cat in the new menu,' she laughed.

Mavis breathed a sigh of relief.

'The hygiene people did have a problem with that, of course, but they think that the new company is using out of date stock, which might explain the illnesses.'

*Limoncello – Perry A. Simpson*

Brenda glanced back at Mavis, 'Did you say that Dave was doing the new meals on wheels?'

'Yes,' Mavis snapped. 'I know that your thinking Dave has something to do with this?'

'The four most beautiful words in our common language, I told you so.'

Mavis looked offended, 'For your information Dave is just a driver.

'Do you honestly think they would trust him to be in charge of kitchen with his track record?' Maggie added.

'True, but now you know the reason for the excessive use of those spices.'

⁓⁕⁓

'Dave you are free to go.'

Dave lifted his head from his folded arms and looked up at the young female officer. 'What about the body?'

'Our inquiry is ongoing, but it appears that body was that of a cleaner who had gone missing two days ago. They think he was helping himself a couple of chops and was accidentally shut in the freezer unit. He was there all weekend, that's why they didn't find him until today. You were not at work the day he was shut in the freezer.'

Dave knew that it must have been him. He popped in to pick up his Manchester United scarf and was in too much of hurry to get home to watch the match. He noticed the freezer door was open, grabbed a couple of ready meals for his mother and closed it behind him before slipping out the emergency exit door.

It was an emergency – the game had already started.

*Limoncello – Perry A. Simpson*

## The Bricklayer

Patricia Cunningham was troubled by the contents of the file she was reviewing. She didn't really know what it was exactly that was bothering her, but it had a similar tone to the level crossing claim almost a year ago.

The tortoise-shell eyed brunette with a figure that, not only was now constantly source admiring looks from the opposite sex, but she was now in charge of all the complex claims at Pearson Insurance Brokers. It was a promotion resulting her handling the level crossing saga. She had successfully uncovered the mystery behind the letter, which had been the key to understanding and resolving the various claims. This new case too, had similarities, but involved only one claimant, Mr Frank O'Sullivan. A letter from him, had been recently added to the file, just as in the other case and it was the letter that eventually settled the case.

Patricia opened the file and neatly laid the contents across her desk in a chronological order. This always started with the claimants form F9, which she placed to the far left. She noted that there was a incident report from the site health and safety representative. As this was a work related incident, the police had been called and this report therefore was earlier than that of the representative's. There was a series of photographs, some gruesome ones that made Patricia flinch. There was no report, a certificate, a statement or a letter from the hospital. Patricia knew only too well that this information may need to be provided to support the plaintiff's claim. Most requests for information presented no problem but occasional difficulties did arise. Such difficulties could include conflicts of interest, unreasonable expectations about the information the attending doctor may hold. In this case a medical report would be necessary to clarify the plaintiff's position in terms of any advanced patient care needed, ongoing illness as an entitlement or excusing factor for sickness benefit claims and fitness of occupation. Glancing through the photos, it would seem that Frank's claim would involve all of these Patricia concluded.

Now she turned her attention to the letter on the Pearson Insurance Brokers letterhead paper with a request for additional details in relation to sections three, eight and nine.

'Now, I see why this case has ended up with me. There are quite a few pieces of the puzzle still needed,' She pondered.

'Frank's claim is not supported with any medical information from the A&E department and all we have is some photographs, a couple of versions of what is thought to have happened and a letter from the plaintiff, Frank, himself. She unfolded the slightly crumpled letter.

It had been hand written.

He has unusually neat handwriting for a builder, she thought. Looking at the date of the letter she assumed that this was written as a response to the request made by the insurance company.

She began to read the contents of the letter.

"Dear Sir/Madam,

I am writing in response to your request for additional information in relation to sections 3, 8 and 9 of the accident report form.

For section 3, I put "piss poor planning" as the cause of my accident.

For section 8 you asked for a more detailed explanation to account for the injuries that I suffered in sections 9. I trust the following detailed explanation will be sufficient.

I was working alone on the roof of a new multi-story building. When I completed my work, I found that I had some bricks left over, but far too many to carry down by hand. So, I decided to lower them in an empty blue water barrel using a pulley system, mounted on the side of the building on the sixth floor.

The rope was secured at ground level and I went up onto the roof, swung the barrel out and loaded the bricks into it. Then I went down and untied the rope, holding it tightly to ensure a slow descent of the bricks, but to my surprise I found myself being jerked off the ground. It happened so quickly, that I forgot to let go of the rope and continued my journey up the side of the building at an uncontrollable rate.

When I reached the third floor, I came into contact with the barrel travelling downwards at an equally impressive speed, resulting in a fractured skull, minor abrasions and the broken collarbone, as listed in section 9 of the accident report form.

I came to a sudden stop when my knuckles rammed against the pulley block. At the same time the barrel of bricks hit the ground and the bottom fell out of the barrel.

Now devoid of the weight of the bricks, I began an

*Limoncello – Perry A. Simpson*

uncontrolled rapid descent, down the side of the building, still gripping the rope. I met the barrel again coming up around the third floor, resulting in two fractured ankles, a broken tooth and several lacerations of my legs and lower body, as listed in section 9 of the accident report form.

The brief and painful encounter with the broken barrel slowed me enough to reduce the impact when I landed on a pile of bricks. Only two vertebrae were cracked, as listed in section 9 of the accident report form.

Barely conscious, in pain, and unable to move, I watched the empty barrel beginning its journey back down to join me on the pile of bricks, resulting in the two broken legs, as listed in section 9 of the accident report form.

I trust this clarifies your questions."

The letter was signed "Frank O'Sullivan"

―∞―

Patricia wiped the tears from her eyes with a tissue having read Frank's colourful account of what had happened.

Looking back at section 9 of the form F9, 'Did he really sustain all these injuries?'

She decided to call the hospital and visit Frank and obtain a copy of his medical report.

―∞―

She arrived in the main reception of the hospital and was directed to the ward where Frank was recovering from his horrific catalogue of injuries.

'Hi, my name is Patricia Cunningham, from Pearson Insurance. I am dealing with his accident insurance claim.'

The nurse nodded, but continued to prepare some medication.

'Is it possible to get a copy of his notes?'

'You'll need to speak with his attending.'

'Can I talk with Frank?'

'That might be difficult at the moment.'

'Why?'

'He's been in a coma since they brought him in to A&E.'

Patricia was dumbstruck.

She glanced through the tiny glass window.

Frank lay on the bed, motionless, connected to the outside world by a complex arrangement of medical equipment, pipes and tubing.

Patricia glanced down at his file in her hand. It was déjà vu. The similarity between this case and the level crossing saga was frightening. She compared the signature on the letter with that on the original policy document. They were the same – No Doubt. How the hell did he file this claim?

*Limoncello – Perry A. Simpson*

# *Squash*

'Well done Tommy my boy. I am impressed with how you have raised your game this week.'

'Patronising sod,' Thomas snapped, throwing his racket on the floor.

It was true he had worked hard on his game all week, but for one momentary lapse in concentration, he would have beaten Steve on the squash court today. He knew it was only a matter of time before victory would be his.

Thomas Palmer and his friend, Steve Plummer had decided that for their next weekend away they are going to take on the Lyke Wake Walk, a 40-mile hike across the North Yorkshire Moors.

In preparation for this Steve has decided that they needed to play squash.

Thomas, being more practically minded had his reservations regarding their preparation for such an endurance challenge. To make things worse he had some black T-shirts printed with the slogan, "Happiness is hiking with friends' in bold lettering across the chest.

༺❀༻

Thomas adjusted the water temperature, tested it with his hand before jumping underneath the power jets. Steve had already started his tedious beautification routine.

'Are you sure playing squash is enough for the Lyke Wake Walk?" Thomas asked, seizing the opportunity.

'Of course, it's only a 40-mile hike.'

'Yes, a 40-mile challenge walk across the highest and widest part of the North York Moors National Park in North-East Yorkshire.'

'You worry too much Tommy boy. It'll be a doddle.'

'So you know how to read an ordinance survey map and use a compass then?'

'There will be plenty of signs.'

'What about breaking in our boots?'

'You just need to soak them in a bucket of water over night.'

'What about food? It's not a stroll in the park, Steve.'

'We'll have lunch at The Lion at Blakey. A couple bottles of water should be all we need.'

'It sounds like you've got this all worked out.'

'Almost.'

Thomas wasn't convinced that Steve had worked out all the details. What he did know from his research is that this was a long walk across very difficult terrain. Thomas was well aware that this was going to be another one of those nightmare weekends.

He decided to leave Steve to finish off his routine, turned the tap off, wrapped his damp towel round his waist and headed for the locker area. Steam hung just beneath the low ceiling.

Several other gym fanatics were getting ready to join the other hamsters the tread mills or brutalise their bodies on the assortment of torture machines.

Thomas had to admit he hated gyms.

Steve was singing, badly, bringing smiles across to the faces of others in the changing room.

A phone rang, but just ignored it. He wasn't going to take a call in the changing room.

The phone rang again and this time the caller was much more persistent. He quickly retrieved the mobile from the locker and hit the send button.

*Limoncello – Perry A. Simpson*

'Hello,' he whispered into the phone.

'Honey, It's me. Are you still at the club?' the voice on the other end bleated out.

Thomas had accidentally turned on the hands-free on the phone.

'Yes,' he replied sheepishly, looking up at the curious ear wiggers who were now focused on him.

'Great! I am at the shopping centre. I saw a beautiful new suit. Just right to go with my new job. It's absolutely gorgeous! Can I buy it?'

'Mmm.'

'It's half price?'

'Mmm.' Thomas glanced up to a sea of smirking on-lookers.

It's only £200.00'

'Mmm.'

A couple about to go off to play squash started to chuckle.

'Please darling. Do you fancy an early night too tonight? I'll wear the sexy red lingerie you bought me. You know, the one you bought me that has extra holes. It will make your Lord Nelson stand to attention.,' she giggled.

Thomas was now blushing, well aware that the build-in hands free feature was broadcasting his conversation to a captive audience in the changing room.

'Mmm.'

'Yes. Do you want the full works?'

'Mmm.'

'Oh, is it awkward to talk?'

The room erupted into laughter.

Thomas couldn't believe that he was sharing this intimate conversions was with a room full of complete strangers. His embarrassment obvious for all to see.

'Ahhh and I also stopped at Crown Motors today.'

'Mmm.'

'Well, I thought I will need a better car for my new job.'

*Limoncello – Perry A. Simpson*

'Mmm.'

Thomas just wanted this conversation to end or for the eager audience to disperse. This conversation had gone viral.

'What do you think to a lovely little pink Vauxhall Corsa?'

'Mmm.'

'It's got sixteen valves. Nice little sports seats with pink stripes. Oh, and really good mirrors. It'll be my new little pink pussy wagon.'

Thomas frowned. He could not believe he was having this conversation – in public – amongst complete strangers.

On a scale of one to ten, this had to be an eleven for embarrassing moments. Beads of sweat were clearly visible on his pale forehead. His cheeks were a shade of fireman's red.

'The man in the show room, Derek, was very nice. He can do us a great part-ex deal for the Metro.'

'Mmm.'

'Are you OK? You're not saying very much.'

'Mmm.'

'No one can hear this conversation, can they?'

The audience erupted into laughter once more.

'Sorry love. You should have said. I must be embarrassing you?'

'Mmm.'

'Well, he will give us 5K for the part-ex?'

There was a gasp in the locker room.

'£5,000 for what?' Steve asked as emerged from the steamy haze of the shower room.

'OK, sweetie. I'll see you later. I love you.'

The audience cheered and clapped.

'Who was that?'

Thomas handed the mobile phone to a very confused looking Steve.

*Limoncello – Perry A. Simpson*

'It's Gillian your wife.'

The audience in the changing room erupted into uncontrollable laughter.

Realising what Thomas has just done, he snatched the phone from him, furiously pressing the buttons on the phone to turn off the hands free.

'See you Thursday.' Thomas grinned, tossed his sports bag over his shoulder and left.

*Limoncello – Perry A. Simpson*

## The Coin Trick

A year ago, Jack Fischer had saved the life of a man, Harry Bannister, who had done the very same ten years earlier. In a strange sort of way this had been pay back for his act of bravery.

One year on and his life had fallen apart. He was separated and arguing over access rights to his son, Peter.

A year ago Jack was full of hope and optimism, today he only felt doubt and despair. He hadn't seen this coming. There were no obvious signs. No arguments. Nothing.

Until a year ago, his wife, Gillian had been a rock, a loyal, devoted and committed mother.

'What happened? What did I do wrong?' he grimaced.

'Now, she has a new man in her life and I only get to see Peter on the Sundays.'

⁂

The sky was filled with a dynamic mosaic of blue as the fluffy white clouds raced across the sky.

Jack looked out the window to see little Peter getting out of the car. Peter charged into the restaurant, excitement spread across his little white face,

'Dad. I have some new coin tricks to show you.'

Gillian waved to Jack and quickly left.

'Great. We will eat first and then you can show me. How does that sound?'

'Oh, alright.'

Peter was never very adventurous with his food and it was the usual Chicken Goujons, chips and baked beans.

Jack watched Peter playing with his food and remembered that very memorable day they all spent at the beach. How recalled how Peter had repeatedly walked to the water's edge to collect water in his leaky bucket only to find it was empty when he reached his sand castle.

It was also that night he met the man who had saved his life.

The weather turned suddenly, just as his marriage did. One minute the sun was shining, the air warm and comfortable. The world was a wonderful place and life was full of happiness.

Today, like every other day is a rainy day. There was a permanent cold chill in the air, a constant reminder, not to get too comfortable in life because the world can be a cruel place where life can be full of doom and gloom.

'Dad, can I show you my tricks now?'

'When you've finished your dinner.'

'Mark lets me show him any time.'

This was one of those moments he had been dreading. The comparison between the real father and the newly adopted one. 'Peter, if we were at home then that would be different, but we are in a restaurant and we should eat our food first.'

'OK.' Peter tucked into the remainder of his meal, swinging his legs under his chair.

Jack caught the eye of a very attractive woman entering the restaurant. He watched as she took her place at the table opposite.

She had shoulder length auburn hair, hazel eyes, framed with black oval-shaped glasses. She was wearing spray on blue brushed denim trousers, a baggy cream mohair jumper and a brown Gucci bag.

*Limoncello – Perry A. Simpson*

She smiled at him.
Jack smiled back.

༺❀༻

'I've finished Dad.'

Jack was somewhere else for that moment, but returned again to look at Peter.

He hadn't eaten all of his chips, but he would let him off.

'OK Peter, what have you got for me?'

A huge smile ripped across Peter's little face and his eyes lit up as excitement bubbled inside him. He took out a £1 coin from his pocket.

'Watch carefully Dad. I am going to pass this coin through my hand. First, I have to find my soft spot.'

Peter gentle pressed the coin in several locations on the back of his left hand. 'There it is. Now I will push it through my hand.'

The coin appeared to pass through his hand, dropping onto the table.

'Wow, that's amazing. How did you that.'

Peter smiled, but wasn't going to let on. He took out four very shiny coins from his pocket and placed them on the table.

'Now I am going to attempt a juggling feat.'

Jack watched as Peter turned his palms upwards and placed a single coin in each before closing his hands.

'Can you place a coin on each on my fingers Daddy?'

'What? Like this?'

'Yes. Now, I will attempt to flip my hands over and catch the other two coins.'

Peter flipped his hands over and the two coins fell onto the table.

'Missed. Can you place the coins on my hands again dad?'

*Limoncello – Perry A. Simpson*

## The Coin Trick

Jack obligingly did so.

Peter flipped his hands over this time and caught all the coins.

'Well done Peter.'

Peter opened his right hand to reveal only one coin, followed by his left hand which contained three coins.

'Wow, Peter how did you do that?'

Several people started to clap, including the attractive lady opposite.

Pleased with himself Peter wanted show off his next trick.

'Dad do you have paper money?'

Jack took out a £5 note from his wallet and placed it on the table.

'Now, I am going balance this coin on this note.'

Peter very carefully folded the note in half. Then he opened it slightly and placed a coin face down at the fold. He slowly opened the note. The coin remained balanced on the edge of the fully opened paper note.

People start clapping.

Peter smiled.

'Do you think I can balance these four coins on this note?'

Peter this time balanced the four coins on the paper note.

Just as he started to lift and unfold the note, a waiter accidentally bumped into the table, sending the coins flying into air. One coin dropped into Peter's mouth.

*～∞～*

Peter gasped for air. He couldn't breathe. Jack could see that he was trying to say something, but couldn't talk. Peter's eyes filled with tears. He started to turn a pale shade of blue.

*Limoncello – Perry A. Simpson*

## The Coin Trick

Panic spread throughout the restaurant.

The waiter rushed to call for the emergency services.

People gathered watching Jack hopelessly holding onto Peter.

'Out of the way.'

The attractive lady from the table opposite barged through the crowd, snatched Peter from Jack and turned him round.

'When a child is choking it means that an object, in this case a coin, is stuck in the trachea, keeping air from flowing normally into or out of the lungs.'

Jack just nodded.

'The trachea is usually protected by a small flap of cartilage called the epiglottis. They share an opening at the back of the throat and the epiglottis acts like a lid, snapping shut over the trachea when we swallow. It allows food to pass down the oesophagus, but should prevent it from going down the trachea.'

Jack nodded awkwardly.

She held Peter from behind and thrust her abdominal into his back, 'This is known as Heimlich manoeuvre.'

The coin flew into the air and Jack caught it.

'This is what happens when something goes down the wrong pipe.'

There were gasps from onlookers around the room.

'Thank you miss. How can I ever repay you.'

'It was nothing – Really. Smart boy.'

'That was amazing. Are you a doctor?'

'Not exactly. My work does involve working with people and money.'

Jack looked confused.

'I work for the Inland Revenue.' She smiled.

*Limoncello – Perry A. Simpson*